CW01507426

POEMS FROM AN ATTIC

ALSO BY IRIS MURDOCH

FICTION
Under the Net
The Flight from the Enchanter
The Sandcastle
The Bell
A Severed Head
An Unofficial Rose
The Unicorn
The Italian Girl
The Red and the Green
The Time of the Angels
The Nice and the Good
Bruno's Dream
A Fairly Honourable Defeat
An Accidental Man
The Black Prince
The Sacred and Profane Love Machine
A Word Child
Henry and Cato
The Sea, The Sea
Nuns and Soldiers
The Philosopher's Pupil
The Good Apprentice
The Book and the Brotherhood
The Message to the Planet
The Green Knight
Jackson's Dilemma

NON-FICTION
Sartre: Romantic Rationalist
Acastos: Two Platonic Dialogues
Metaphysics as a Guide to Morals
Existentialists and Mystics

POEMS FROM AN ATTIC

Selected Poems, 1936–1995

Iris Murdoch

*Edited by Anne Rowe, Miles Leeson, Rachel Hirschler
and Frances White*

With an introduction by Sarah Hall

*Dear Avril
with love and thanks
for your many words
of wisdom!*

Anne x

Chatto & Windus
LONDON

1 3 5 7 9 10 8 6 4 2

Chatto & Windus, an imprint of Vintage, is part of the
Penguin Random House group of companies

Vintage, Penguin Random House UK, One Embassy Gardens,
8 Viaduct Gardens, London SW11 7BW

penguin.co.uk/vintage
global.penguinrandomhouse.com

First published by Chatto & Windus in 2025

Typeset in 11/14pt Minion Pro by Six Red Marbles UK, Thetford, Norfolk
Printed and bound in Great Britain by Clays Ltd, Elcograf S.p.A.

The authorised representative in the EEA is Penguin Random House Ireland,
Morrison Chambers, 32 Nassau Street, Dublin D02 YH68

A CIP catalogue record for this book is available from the British Library

ISBN 9781784746124

Penguin Random House is committed to a sustainable future
for our business, our readers and our planet. This book is made
from Forest Stewardship Council® certified paper.

In memory of Audi Bayley (1942–2024) with gratitude for her generosity and many kindnesses to Murdoch scholarship

Contents

Poems 1952–1958

Conversations with a Prince c. 1963
Declaration

Encounter

Absence

Conversations with a Prince

Remembrance

Poems 1972–1995

Introduction

Dear Reader.

Imagine it for a moment. The attic.

A steep staircase up, with narrow gauge steps and close walls. Or a pull-down ladder, perhaps, standing almost vertically after it's been tugged and shuttled down and has arrested on the floor, the handrail an essential grip to help you climb. There's a dark void above your head, and cool draughts of air breathe from its entrance. There's a whiff of mustiness, aging storage, long-held secrets. This attic holds literary gold, stashed in a private oak chest, and you've been invited into the story of its discovery.

So you ascend.

Up in the vault there are architectural-grade cobwebs, brushing against your cheek. Spiders hide behind sacks of envenomated prey as you switch on the lights – a few single overhead bulbs, buzzing and tinking, casting weak luminescence into the darkness. If you like, imagine no electricity to help you see, only shafts of bright Oxford daylight filtering through gaps in the roof, spokes radiating – as fatefully as cinematic illumination – towards a dark wooden trove.

The attic's diminutive space is packed with bric-a-brac and artefacts: old suitcases, desiccated magazine bundles, boxes of clothes – dagger-collared shirts, woollens, tunics – broken clocks and paintings, things tipping and teetering in all directions. There's the slightly sour lime and dust smell of avian and rodent activity. Perhaps you want to hear a very English, cast-iron bell sounding across the city. Perhaps the scuttering of claws on the roof coping or inside the walls, mice, shrews. A crow cackling from the gable end, a sound moderately and appropriately gothic for this subject.

And there it is. The chest, once half-hidden by life's archived detritus, is now revealed: it's waiting for you, sitting squat as a prophet in a clearing, because you already know what you're looking for up here, whose house this was and what treasure awaits you.

But what kind of chest is it – a hope, a casket, a blanket? Panelled, utilitarian or bracketed and footed, storing linen or guns or grain before her notebooks? Is there an old-fashioned bow key to turn in the lock – its mechanism still slick and perfectly functional – before the heavy lid can be raised? Imagine the moment of revelation however you wish, but one thing is certain – the sheer, exhilarating thrill of finding the unpublished poems of Iris Murdóch.

Now, if you don't want to leave the reverie of re-enacted discovery, sit up here in the attic on a stack of old newspapers or the wobbling remains of a stool, with the candid little creatures and the floating dust, and flick through the notebooks. You'll have to make head and tail of the handwriting, the crossings out, the additions, the versions, but you will see how artistic the edits were, how earnestly she crafted her pieces over the years. Let's say the best editions will become apparent, in the way of epiphanic plots, their text lifting out towards you like magic-eye pictures. Or, if you are satisfied by your vicarious attic adventure and your haul, retreat, climb back down into the real world. Sit with this book in a comfortable armchair in your own home, or on your commute to work, glancing up to see a fellow traveller reading a novel with a familiar cover – yes, one of hers – or sit in your favourite café while cups and saucers chink and friends gossip, and read an extraordinary collection of poetry.

You're probably curious. Why were these works sequestered and held back for so long? Something explosive, scandalous or sacred in them, maybe. Are they confessions? Or are they off-cuts and under-makes – lesser somehow than her established literary pedigree warrants? What might be expected of one of the leading novelists of the twentieth century, a decorated titan of fiction, when it comes to a 'secondary' discipline? A trained classical scholar. A philosopher. A woman who was the target of identity politics for decades, parts of her nature closeted then exposed, speculated upon, judged, as women are, for her passions, her proclivities and her relationships, as well as her work. She's been the subject of biopics, biographies, countless dissertations. She's familiar to you, known, intriguing, still somewhat mysterious.

Iris Murdoch was a writer of formidable and industrious intellect, playfully mischievous around taboos; she was extremely concerned with concepts of goodness, wickedness, our human affect, and her work was immune to the fashions of fiction. Throughout the novels there are gothic and mystical tropes, conundrums, sublimations, scenarios that tease and test morality. Characters languishing, hiding in plain sight, hopeful for things not happening – perhaps we might call them 'star-fishers', like the girl in her youthful poem. If her published stories do not wear the personal overtly, will her poems bring you closer to an innermost self, a private source, aspects of Iris not previously disclosed on the page? Is this thing in your hands a *Liber Veritatis*?

Truth. That jinking will-o'-the-wisp, that slippery, shapeshifting charmer.

'Honesty is a hard thing,' Murdoch notes in these pages, though she does nevertheless hope to be tethered, as 'truth's prisoner in the end'. How tempting to want to get at the heart of a writer, find what makes her heart tick. Especially a writer with such vast talent, status and persona, with quite complicated dramas around her life. Her observation does beg the question – within the construct of words, might we ever really trap truth, arrest its flight, interrogate and hold it to account? A novelist must have persuasive command of language and extensive representative abilities, so as to convince readers of believable virtual worlds, a realistic cast and viable propositions. Is a poet more able to dispense with the makery-uppery of long form, distil subjects to essence, pin a thing truly?

Again, Murdoch can guide on this matter. Her poems are often beautifully formal songs, sonnets, ballad templates, tight in composition and following structural rules, rhyme and rhythm. They take in traditions, her nationalities, poetic legacies, and in doing so they often act as sprung, performative devices, tricksy boxes of ideas and emotions. As she herself states, they 'play a game to tell the truth'.

Which is not to say there isn't a wincing, or thrilling, intimacy to them, depending on how you're minded. They are both frank and withholding; they are contradictory, complicated, like she was (like you are, and I am). In her poems, she seems to be trying to work her life and her self out, sometimes physically, sometimes politically, to 'process', as we might say now. But they do not seem overly therapeutic, and they completely resist solipsism, the deep well of me-ism. They are neither salacious nor gnomic, but pitched between poles, a territory where she must have felt able to confide and still be mindful. Encoded or openly, they often address her lovers – those both desired and achieved, unconsummated and resisted – as well as her spouse. They include her troublesome liaisons, relationships that vexed and damaged as well as elated her. Anguish, despair, longing, bonding. The many sensations of a lover are held in these lines. There's the struggle and occasional reconciliation with more difficult feelings, of guilt, lust, despair, heartsickness, possessiveness – a poem can be a strongbox, the perfect receptacle for such live emotional demons. Touching, and not being able to touch another body. Lovelorn states, anger and torment. The violence and darkness and reckoning of desire. She stows it all in wordy oubliettes – quite literally these poems resided for a long time in a place of forgetting.

There are also gentle communion poems, celebrating the safe ports and companionability of home and husband. Poems written for women she held relationships with, or wanted to, are especially ardent, complex, tender and gorgeous. These read not like imprisoned offences but more as vulnerable documents, wishes blown softly towards those who fascinated her, or away, released.

It is quite the poetic toolkit. Her range of tones is, in fact, remarkable – strident, self-effacing, humorous, deadly serious, god-stung, entreating, ironic. In places, there's baroque gender wrangling, meditation on self and sexual reassignment. This, in an age well before open public discourse on non-binary existence, identity fluidity, bisexuality and polyamory, the assurances of orientation. Perhaps you might sense, though, that even if these distinctions had been available to her, she may not have adopted them, but rather would have continued to embrace the versatile, surprising, unclassifiable natures of identification. For all you might pass through a few more layers towards her core via this work, that core remains categorically protean.

While there is a very broad spectrum of expression, experience and interaction within Murdoch's poetry, one central and fundamental energy, one character, keeps showing up. Love. Love is embodied. The poet frequently meets and communicates and even grapples with Love, who goes about the pages in semi-corporeal, semi-deified form, charging the poet, helping the poet, hindering the poet. A gatekeeper, a gamekeeper. A rider, a drowning oceanic creature. Masked. Bemused. Almost avenging. Love jokes and judges; it is instructive, lawyerly, sparring, waiting roadside like a ragged oracle or appearing as a rescuer after a fall. Love becomes more significant than a lover, even. Submitting to the truth of feelings, to the emotion and power and meaning it brings, if not to a human candidate, is in a way the ultimate truth to be found within this book, should one still be needed. It is the collection's colophon.

Wherever and however Murdoch might be located in the writing, the writing itself is wonderful, animate and effective, creating spaces that are visual and sensual and experiential, as you might expect. The skill with which she writes verse is undeniable. She has an ear for music, understands cadence and verbal acrobatics. She might produce work that is blunt cut, or she might feather. She retains the novelist's gift for narrative quickening and landscaping, atmospherics, activation of scene and scenario, and she applies these skills to poetic forms.

She is, aside from everything else, an exceptional nature writer, going toe-to-toe with heavyweight pastoralists, the rugged rural bards that were her contemporaries, producing lines so well observed and imagistically rendered you might assume it was her day job, rather than auxiliary. Murdoch's 'Fox' – that seemingly requisite topic of all twentieth-century British nature poets – equals any other poemy fox in the annals. It is sudden and brilliant. She is superb at weather, a 'segment of rainbow . . . still in action', and trees, pine boughs 'damp with resin, dry with cones, rustling like rising bones'. The sea provides a female reliquary, a 'wave-washed bone-white' shell whose 'tender hinge' becomes downright erotic.

The 'strong and skilful strokes' of her Diver, from the 'Juvenilia' section of the collection, might well be a description of her own technical ability with a pen in the making of the poems you now hold. What can clearly be ascertained, from her early attempts through to those written later in life, is an astonishing talent, which she nurtured, and humbled, and hid, but did not abandon. Though draft after draft may have been kept aside, reservedly, none are unworthy of her hand or her mind, none are mediocre.

Yes, perhaps when you finish reading and close this book, you might feel a little closer to Iris. You might feel satisfied or edified or disquieted by having had additional access to her personal life, revelations about her heart, and the hearts of those in her romantic orbit. There may be verification of her relationships here, records in the library of lovers and friends, intimate glimpses of her ways of being and relating.

But don't forget, poems play games to tell the truth; no singular soul or definition of personality can be found in this literary form, or perhaps in any other. All writing is a version of veracity, isn't it, no matter how moving or permissive or authentic? Who among us, dear reader, can be fixedly known by what we write, and place discreetly in the attic?

Sarah Hall, 2025

Editors' note on the text

This anthology has been compiled principally from the poems contained in ten poetry notebooks and the typescript entitled *Conversations with a Prince* found in the attic of Iris Murdoch's home in Oxford in 2016. All these materials are now held in the Iris Murdoch Collections in Kingston University Archives and are available to view by appointment by contacting archives@kingston.ac.uk. Two copies of the *Conversations with a Prince* typescript are also deposited in the Brotherton Library at the University of Leeds.

Murdoch dated her early poems with the day, month and year in which they were composed, while later poems are identified only by year. This collection largely follows a chronological order with a few poems not in strict sequence to allow those that complement each other to be placed together. Poems are listed by title or, if untitled, by all or part of the first line of the poem in quotation marks. Italics have been used for words that were underlined by Murdoch herself for emphasis.

The *Conversations with a Prince* section of this collection is dated circa 1963, the year Murdoch sent the typescript that contained these poems to her editor, Norah Smallwood, at Chatto & Windus. However, the poems were written during the 1950s and revised over a number of years. One additional poem, 'I Overcome Love', was taken from a notebook and added to this section as it clearly resembles the style and content of the sonnets included there.

When Murdoch includes a dedication, she usually writes 'for' with the dedicatee's initials added. She also notes that some poems were written 'with' a person, and we believe that these were composed either in the company of that person or were inspired by them. Perhaps for reasons of discretion, no dedications appear in the *Conversations with a Prince* typescript, but if one is included in her notebook version of the poem, we have reinstated it here.

For clarity, the name of each dedicatee appears below the poem title in brackets. Murdoch did not include a dedication to Elizabeth

Anscombe alongside the poem, 'The dear and detailed dream of your carved head' but research evidence suggests strongly that Anscombe is Murdoch's intended subject. Similarly, references to various other inspirations for poems have been placed below the title. Further brief biographies and relevant background information to the poems can be found in the end notes.

We have included what we believe to be the most skilful version of each poem with as much sensitivity and accuracy as possible. Previously published poems are either taken from the original publications, or a notebook version if we believe they are more accomplished.

Poems from an Attic

*'In the poetry I am trying to change my old wicked god
into a good god but to change our gods
we have to change ourselves'*

Iris Murdoch's journal, 1959

Juvenilia 1936–1939

The Diver

His dark, lithe form gleams wet with salty drops
As on the green sea-verge for breath he stops.
Then clambering on a dry out-jutting ledge
With dripping feet, he poises on the edge,
Then cleaves the cold blue waves in milky foam.
His dusky form a moment can been seen,
A vague dark shadow, merging into green;
While he with open eyes swims silently
Along the weedy floor of the dim sea,
An eager searcher 'neath the azure dome.

With strong and skilful strokes he makes his quest
Along the ocean floor, his limbs caressed
By slimy sea plants and by soft sea flowers
Whose tangled beauty floats in watery bowers –
And fishes, silvery-finned, pass staring by.
He reaches out towards a patch of white
Which glistens dully in the greenish light . . .
At last with bursting lungs he upward speeds
'Mid crystal bubbles to the air he needs,
And gulps and gasps beneath the sunny sky.

Then, swimming in to rest on shining sands,
He tries to open with his dusky hands
The silvery oyster shell; tears it apart
With trembling, bleeding fingers, till the heart
Its pearly treasure trove reluctant yields.
Then breathless does the bright-eyed diver gaze

As still beside the laughing waves he stays,
And feasts his eyes upon the glancing pearl
Enshrined and cradled in its silver shell –
Then turns and hurries back across the fields.

Catkins

Down in the fields the winter holds its breath.
Cold quietness embalms the wood.
Last autumn's tawny beech leaves clothe the earth
Yet in a still soft shroud.
Let not a word be spoken – Nature's bowed
Her lovely head, and sleeps a sleep like death.

But look where in the frozen glen
The saucy catkins toss their tasselled tails.
No solemn quietness for them,
They sing of life and spring again.

To M.S.

She doesn't know I love her – for I hide
My love under a casual friendship.
She cannot feel it burning in my hands
When I touch her cool white hands.
She cannot see it blazing in my eyes
When I look into her calm grey eyes.
She cannot hear it trembling in my voice
When I speak to her. She will never know
My love – and never love me. Yet she gives
Me bright gifts unconsciously.

'The heavy purple hyacinth'

The heavy purple hyacinth breathes out
Its sleepy fragrance – and I sit alone
Reading Euripides, and waiting while
The slow cramped-cruel watch-hands creep around
To mark the hour when letters come from him.

Star-Fisher

There was a young lady whose
    Chief occupation
Was fishing for stars in the
    Milky Way.
With bluebottle eyes and a
    Sense of vocation
She dangled her legs on the
    Banks of the day.
With touching affection her
    Uncles and cousins
Would come every Friday to
    Bait all her hooks,
They sat on the bank in their
    Scores and their dozens
With red velvet gaiters and
    Cookery books.

Her three elder sisters and
    Ravid relations
Were all much too haughty to
    Help with the rest,
But when she had sent them some
    Choice constellations,
On Collyfrock's Day they would
    Knit her a vest.

But the one she liked best in her
      Family Circle
Was Grandfather Gangle, with
      Garrible ears,
Down slippery skies he would
      Slide to encircle
Her wishoppy waist and half
      Drown her in tears.

And when they had had some un-
      Usually rousing
Astronomal liquor in
      Fuliginous pails,
They deafened the stars with their
      Noisy carousing
And tied cauliflowers to the
      Comets' bright tails.

Before the 2nd of April – to James

I love you now, before we've even met.
Or is it some dream you, not you at all?
Am I entangled in a shadowy net
Of phantasy? And shall it fall
To earth in tearful ruin, the bright tall
Tower of dreams I've built? Be swift, my dear,
And lay a gentle hand upon my fear.

After the 2nd of April

Forgive me, dear, that for an hour,
I let my fancies blind me.
Brief was the summer of that flower –
And now I leave behind me
A broken-wingèd dream that could not rise
And memories of the agony in your eyes.

To Kathleen ni Houlihan

I would go back to Ireland,
Over the white sea-foam,
To the dreaming hills of Ireland
And the little green fields of home.
To the streets of Dublin city,
And the land where I belong –
And my heart will break with pity,
When I think upon her wrong.

I will go back to Ireland,
To the beautiful misty isle –
The land of gods and heroes
Where even grief will smile.
And her brow is white with sorrow,
And her dearest sons are dead –
But she knows that her tomorrow
Holds a bright crown for her head.

I will go back to Ireland,
To the land of Deirdre's grief,
Where the sorrow of a thousand years
Is yet without relief.
But her eyes are bright with courage,
Though her heart is dark with pain,
And in the hour of agony
We'll pledge our hearts again.

Ballad

There was a young lady who had yellow hair
(The wind blows the seeds of the poppy away)
She rode through my land on a snowy white mare.
(The wind blows the seeds of the poppy away)
With spurs on her ankles and whip in her hand,
She galloped on May-day the length of my land,
And her hair was as bright as the shimmering sand.
(Oh the wind it sighs and it passes)

I never beheld that young lady again
(The wind blows the seeds of the poppy away)
And I searched the green hills and the valleys in vain.
(The wind blows the seeds of the poppy away)
Tho' the blood on her spurs was all gleaming and wet,
The look in her eyes I shall never forget,
And the heart that she stole from me follows her yet.
(O the wind it sighs and it passes)

Reverie in Winchester Cathedral

Chill-grey and gracious arches rise and flow,
And surging stones soar to a dim, rich roof
With interlocking wings.
And then, vibrating low, the organ moans
Foaming in sweet crescendos and its tones
Of shadowed splendour clothe the lily-pale
Virginity of breathless nave and aisle.

I stood in awe and wonder for a while,
In dread of such a silence and such sound –
Till swift and sudden sped
A swallow from the vaulted dark, and passed above my head.
It seemed a spirit – like the Holy Ghost
That beat its dove-wings in far Galilee.
I knelt in peace. Tho' yet the organ rings
Above it still the darkening arches fill
With a merciful murmuring of wings.

To a Girl with Yellow Hair

(whom I met after seeing Eliot's 'Family Reunion')

How is it that we understood each other
At once, and recognised each other
Without the usual preliminaries? Our talk
Was about realities – not an unmeaninged
Beating of lost wings in darkness.
You smiled at me in a mirror and I sighed
At your soon going. Understanding
And the truth that clings
To the side and the heart, the curse
Of vision belongs to few. Kinship
Has here a meaning – let not
Life snap the thread.

Irreparable Loss

Her conversation tinkles on.
Unwinged her words come clinking down
Into my sulky silence like
Sugar-lumps into tea-cups thrown.
They soak and sink. A blunted mind
Breaks the circuiting of thought,
Languidly observes the clock
Labouring through an afternoon.
My passionate escape from Time,
Whose thunder thrilled me, hurrying near,
Forgotten, yawning I subside
Into a carelessness of hours.
Yawn, and sate my hatred on
The tulips pink beside her hand.
Servile and obsequious flowers
Willow down upon her hand.
Bored, I contemplate her face
Eagerly inane of thought,
Mouthing memoried remarks,
Painted on the hollow bone.
Her tongueless talk encounters still
The slow clock's constant counterpoint.
'Alas, Poor Yorick!' And I toss
Blank smiles into her empty skull.

Poems 1940–1948

Afternoon Tea with a Lady

(Eliot, Eliot, Eliot!)

The empty glass clinks down upon the table.
The flowers mist in a corner, slightly dusty;
The clock administrates
The tyranny of time. And I imagine
My martyred blood aflower upon the tablecloth –
Consider weeping loudly – but instead
Study my fingernails and cut the bread.

Behind my right shoulder death
Stands and leans upon me.
I choke. I strain toward life.
The tiger in my hand
Surreptitiously stretches its limbs,
Sinks for a spring, but lies still.
Upon the littered windowsill
The black fly crawls, heavy with summer –
My hand lies, heavy with death.

O save us from the milkman
Who comes at half past nine –
O save us from the curtained pane,
The little trees that stand in line,
The black umbrella in the rain,
Restore to us the bleeding sign
The strong guilt and the stain.

You are the bird that lives in fire,
You have the Midas touch of gold,
White Artemis in the green.
The crenellated suburb street
Dissolves and only heaven's left
And hell and a rope stretched between.
Now at last
My incarcerated soul sings
Sings of the blue and topless voids
Not for its wings.

To P. O'R.

(Patrick O'Regan)

Love at my side sobbed and struck deep –
O honeysuckle hands, so smooth, so sweet –
Far in my flesh pain sits and turns a wheel,
Breaking the aching body of desire.

I bow my head under a green tree –
I crush the broken earth under my knee.
With tight white knuckles I embrace the wood
And try to loose from pain by losing self.

The sky descends in turning spokes of steel –
The stars spin jangling to a final peal –
The earth's wild shrieking at the roots of trees
Dissolves into the crying of a child.

And I am left alone with madman love –
I see his staring eyes in the dark above.
I loose my limbs and droop my head in dust
And give my guilty flesh up to the knife.

Thoughts Around Nash's *Wild Stones*

Hands, hands with blood on them,
Golden wounded hands praying in the dark.
A voice that falls in rings and coils,
A voice that says why why why –
The darkness gives no reply,
Only the roar of falling cities,
Only the moan of night that copulates with night.
I heard a shriek in the wilderness,
Unnatural cries on the downland;
Paul Nash's wild stones are awake
And crying for their flint-eyed young.
A magic bird beats wings of air
Flying to the heart of Max Ernst.
Wine runs in the street,
Wine and blood mixed, reddening the children's feet.
Why these things are I cannot tell,
I, fascinated by red eyes in hell,
While darkness takes to wife its silent bride.

'He gave me a posy'

He gave me a posy of golden oak trees,
A blue wave in a cage,
A whale's eye in a green glass,
And the tired feet of a past age;

The morning's spurs of silver,
The axis of the earth,
The black horns of evening,
The dark hands of birth;

The embryo of a zebra,
The grey girdle of the rain,
The clattering hooves of the mountains
And the little red eyes of pain.

I gave him for guerdon a rosebud,
A sonnet carved on a pearl,
A birch tree's heart in a silver box,
And the pale cold lips of a girl.

Bayswater Tube Station

(suggested by Stanley Spencer's 'Beatitudes of Love')

The dark roof and the line
Glittering thinly with sound, drawing the roar
With terrible crescendo out
Of the gaping corridor. The people
Wait in the preliminary hush,
Leaning or lumped upon seats,
Dimly described by the light
Or footless in the gloomy spaces.
And coldly the light falls upon
The dramatic white of the wall –
The lamp in the corner cuts
Its square of gold on the ground.
The terrible domes of the roof,
The dooming of the glinting girders,
Pregnant to breaking with sound,
Are still arching over our silence.

On a Head from the Acropolis

Within those honeycombs of hair, time
Slept like the water sleeps in a pool
No wind touches or fingers. Stone
Twisted to such a beauty utters a cool
And birdlike speech – the little lace
Intricate curls over the chiselled ears
Are hung, and all the face
Is carved by closeness of its tears.
How madly flung, the centuries that part
You and ourselves lie. Yet that mouth
Crooked with tenderness, a heart
With daring of love's imagination made.
We are amazed at its intelligible truth,
By the sincere stone humble and afraid.

The *Acropolis Korai*

These broken girls the Persians cast in a pit
And roofed them in under the bereaved years.
They slept together, the broken limbs and the faces
And the delicate hands and feet in the crushed dark.
The earth treasured them; and men forgot
The secret of their shuttered places, and lacked
Their loveliness, and left
The sleeping queens under the white hill – but at last
Waking from war into another war
In the thunder of our years they broke the soil and stepped
Starlike into our ashamed world. Welcome
As Persephone, brilliant as Aphrodite, and yet
Wearing the secretive eyes of the maid of Athens.
They were a springtime in stone – the flowers
Anointed with the treasures of their dew
Those shining feet, and the astounded birds
Sang themselves to a silence at the sight
Of the incredible lips, the trembling
Poise and subtle tenderness of mouths, and the knowledge
Strangely stored in a cheek's curve. And we
Hung tortured heads before those broken faces
Hardly able to bear the lovely intense glances,
The eyes where tears stirred in the stone, the sullen,
The sensitive, the tender – taking a quiet
Comfort from the curved arm and the shoulder
Where we could quietly love the simple flesh –
Rejoicing in the curious infinitely
Patient efflorescence of the drapery,

And the formal curls and the delicious
Surge of the braided hair over the pointed breasts.
No words of ours could ever hope to inhabit
The almost merciless purity of those lips –
And the mysterious consciousness that lights
The delicate expanse between the heavy lids
Is dark to us – we have lost
From our ears and our mouths and our ashamed hearts forever
The song they listen to, the world they penetrate,
And the knowledge that carves,
The love that curves their lips.

Chartres Angel

Here is the angel that you strove with, Jacob.
A slender gesture now in the clambering stone,
Pinnacled over the town, footing the air.
The pensive robe hangs innocent of a fold,
The sable shadows pinned upon the shoulder,
While the sunlooking breast is stiff with gold.
The strong enormous wings that beat and beat
In the gasping minute blotting out the sky
Have graciously folded all their hateful length
Intently poised behind the inclining head.
Below and distinct in the shadows, throng
The soaring choirs and companies of saints
Still streaming heavenward. This angel watches
Tall and alone, the town. We can remember
Those hands breaking our life and the clap
Of the hideous wings. The stone has blossomed now
Into a taut silence, pregnant with all terror.

Approach to Belfast

The lough at morning and the ship slipping
In utter silence on the pale blue surface.
The night pulsing in unseen shafts releases
A vessel pallid with light into this coloured space.
The green shores have been made real in the end
Out of continual dreams – and now
I am lapped in the green arms of the island
And all about me is Ireland. The dazzling snow
Of white wings and white walls sails on
In the radiant air and fills
Our eyes. The sky steps off the mountain,
Heavy at edges with a ring of hills.
The red city sighed upon by the smoke
Kneels to tall skylines. Frozen on the rocks
Tense cormorants regard the sidling ship.
Now the water runs in a cleft of docks
And unfalteringly the shining stark arms
Of gantries proclaim the city. The wooden wall meets
Gently, the slow bow as the ship leans
To land in the midst of streets.
Voices and the crash of chains
Daunt the soft heart and make the spirit harden.
The discordant crying of birds and men
Rends for me the gate of the tragic garden.

For D.H. Cairo –

(David Hicks)

When oh my darling the sun sinks
Out of your blue into my golden world
And the sigh of sunset for you
Is the whisper of dawn for me –
I think of you lying asleep
And with warm wings of thought cover
Your body and the dark head
That has no thought of me.

The Fallen Tree

This tree, with its crest of twigs and its body
Of boughs, yearning with green leaves in to the south,
With torn root pours away its detail of glory
Into the deep and undiscriminating earth.
That swaying green and frame of stout gold,
Not long now of colour and of life left,
Supine, a sped hero, has rolled
Sky and cloud downward for the grass to sift.
This flesh of honey, yielding all its odours,
Its separateness, its sap and splendour, up –
Flowers shall crowd the place where each limb moulders,
And fling new beauty on a land that grieves.
The tears of kings are like stars when they drop,
But softly grow into petals and frail leaves.

St James's Park

Inconsequent and casual the gay crowds see
With their thousand eyes the kindly but firm sun
Turn from the London sky. Lingering in a tree
In St James's Park 'Day is done'
It announces to them platitudinously.

The lake is full of golden sky; but under
The banks the iris casts a mauve reflection –
Earlier in the day there was thunder,
And a segment of rainbow is still in action
Over the towers of Whitehall cracked asunder.

The people are constantly coming over the bridge
And the lips of women are red. The sun leaves
A murmuring twilight of people – at the water's edge
A bird complains. The cup of night receives
This rich mixed wine of life, a heady pledge.

The Doves

(St James's Park with Sally)

When the lake, oily with summer colours
Swirled with its green and blues and perhaps a swan,
I have looked up and seen the doves fly down
The void sky with a vibration of the sun.
The doves, black particles falling
Out of a flaming centre, then with a wing
And a breast stricken white, breaking
Suddenly into a new and intermittent morning.
At last white entirely they send
The sun's cry of light for the sky's length
And with heart-beat of wings are sped
Out of my sight, who have seen, who comprehend.

Swiss Winter

No eye forgave. In every deep
Recess, in the windings of the heart
Snow fell and fell. Hands flickered apart
And fell entwined with sleep, fatally locked,
Still cold. And ice on every brow
Glittered a little in the brilliant light.
The beautiful and sequent flow
Of the words, taking their flight
From the talkers' lips, grew thin
In the jumbled mist – and the words
Wavering stupidly in an idle spin
Fell like pierced, like pitiful birds.
Even love in that assembly
Stepped like the torturer from cell to cell –
The neglected door was fortunate to see
Nothing – only sensing the faint smell
Of a corrupt body – heaving the flesh
That cried alone in the dark,
In the frenzied embrace of the lash.

'The dear and detailed dream of your carved head'

The dear and detailed dream of your carved head
Fills all the dim dimensions of my pain.
Your most intent desiring lips and eyes
Brim from the mirror where I ask my name.
This sudden sweet complicity, the Greek
Verse that you told me, all our dear illusion
Turns black between us when we speak
Or act or move to a conclusion.
For I could wish to possess you forever so,
My darling, immobilised in the gesture
Of reaching toward me. Yet I know
That this is to desire your death. Your nature
Being hard and high, you must be set free;
Two secret evil forms will lie enlaced in me.

Poems 1952–1958

Tu es mon mal

(for Wallace Robson)

You have searched my heart; and far down
The dark nets in the dark waters move.
This is but a sad image of love;
Unless from depth itself a strength can come.

Dazzling and electrical, a tension of the nerves,
Fear, and even hatred, turn to steel.
Is this the true tenderness I hoped to feel?
Or is violence itself a power that saves?

I can see no hope in your sex branded eyes.
Our extreme union is a lack of hope.
Is this the future's flesh, its innocent shape,
Kernel of lightning in collapsing skies?

You are the troubled and dark power counter
To which setting foot and knee I strain
Until I define myself in a rending pain
And see in shock my soul's fragments founder.

Shot through the head into a diamond glory.
Promised not present – there is only a shiver
Along the nerves. The notion of never
Is an unformulated part of the story.

Crying with fear compelled from your embrace
You are the steep way that I slowly tread –
The gazing skull that entering my head
Aches with mortality upon my face.

You are the iron man with whom I dance
Where each step is original with life –
While truth is at our wrist like a blunt knife.
You are the wakening as you are the trance.

My hatred for you pierces you like love –
My secret moods come blooded from your heart.
My starry thoughts that burn to fly apart,
Scattering worlds, in your cold orbit move.

There is no escaping the dimensions of space,
All other spaces are contained therein.
You are my necessity; although I run
My thinking feet imagine no new place.

Only the truth can hold our reeling galaxy –
To truth your power must bend its unkind laws.
The Power that holds us both upon our course
Is our unsteady love's only identity.

The darkness in me of untruth to you,
Your jealous force that weighs upon my neck,
Must in our new heaven and earth break
Into the singing of planets the night through.

Our poor love lifts a soiled and bleeding face,
And all the air is black with our offence.
My hand in the darkness touches yours once
And the tenderness I prayed for comes as a grace.

Tu es mon mal oh toi mon guérison,
Tu es la froide terre que reveillaient mes pleurs,
La mort qui me venait combleé de fleurs
Dont le parfum est enfin un bénison.

'The trailing stars tell of dooms'

(for Wallace Robson)

The trailing stars tell of dooms
In a universe next door to ours.
I have seen the fall of the world
Poised at the intricate centre of flowers.
Pretty one, pretty one, I say
To the timid suspense of a cat –
Profound in her enormous eye
A powdery lamp is lit.
Day comes like a settling bird
That I coax to my windowsill –
Reality waits the word
That shall shatter it once and for all.
What a tremulous structure it is,
Focussed, suspended in place
By the random congeries
The atomic form of the face.

Let the personality list
A fraction out of its sense
And the shadows of particles
Will fall with a difference.
Will fall to create new things,
And the colour structure broken
A new born planet sings
That the word has at last been spoken.

'I find that honesty is a hard thing'

(for Wallace Robson)

I find that honesty is a hard thing;
But dappled deception is natural and sweet,
Simple, seductive and most discreet
In the weary grace of its surrendering.
When the sun shines the little birds sing,
And pointed flowers prick my feet,
And I become frisky and fleet
And fly all tedious remembering.
But I hope that nevertheless
I may be most strongly chained and penned
So that although I run with wildness
The tugged at tether will cast me to the ground
Until I have learnt mildness,
Being truth's prisoner in the end.

'You ask a hundred sonnets of me'

(for Wallace Robson)

You ask a hundred sonnets of me – you
That put pain not poetry upon my soul.
The icebergs know the pathway from the pole
That leads them to a mortal rendezvous.
The little ship is crushed and all its crew
Are black and tiny on the sculptured white,
And the finality of freezing night
Touches with treasuring that which is true.
Now the mast totters and the hulls crack
And a cold world enters forever in,
A universe of white that knows no black,
The nightmare strength of ice, the crushing din,
That moves with snowy silence on its track
And softly will obliterate our sin.

'There is no flower'

(for Wallace Robson)

There is no flower on the asking tree
And no foliage at the bottom of the sea.
Only a single bird in the air flying
Is the consolation of our dying.
You are the question that escaped from me,
Finding no answer in our unity.
The cry went out a pilgrim through the earth,
But missed the habitation of the birth.
My heart went straying and returned a deer,
With horns of horror and with eyes of fear.
You, vulnerable to the hunters' darts,
Lay in the dangerous world my other parts.
Where the stars like fireflies are burning in your hair,
And your brow is cut so deep with care
That the bone is reached that has left no blood,
Your eyes contain that minimum of good
That buys back all our paper with its gold;
Unless this story is better left untold,
Or laid by both of us before that Censor
Who may or may not be there,
May or may not answer.

'Opening like the spring your hand dispels'

(for Elias Canetti)

Opening like the spring your hand dispels
The morning mist and shows
The forest glittering like a rose
And the flying echoes
Of great mountains swinging like bells.

Moving with the insistence of fact
Or a dream, your head
Becomes transparent, and I see instead
A city, tiny as a seed,
Distant, precise and intact.

You are never near to me,
Being a thing of distance
Where the movement of romance
Would seem loose and subject to chance;
But your necessity is dear to me.

I am never with you; but roam
The land that is you, and find
There the leaning tree and the kind
Faces of flowers – and mind
A little less being alone.

Even at the extreme place
Where the lines of distance fade
Me, until I am unmade.
There is cool grass where I am laid
And rain upon my face.

In my fragmented eyes
The thousand images collect like drops.
The thunder stops
And upon the new mountain tops
Silence like a thick snow lies.

Now, your footsteps are small and dear,
The mountains kiss your feet
The far distances run to greet
And the submissive waters to meet
You, and the cities draw near.

Now in a nutshell I creep
And like little birds into my
Hands the stars fly.
And like a golden cloud I lie,
And you lie beside me asleep.

The Shell (1)

(with Julian Chrysostomides)

Why no more voices calling from the sea?
I walked this afternoon upon the beach in vain.
I saw salt water birds upon a tree
And they watched, but had no song for me.
Why in this silence is there so much pain?
The slanting sun is whitening the sand.
Beneath the waves the powers patiently
Conjure with love the spirits of the land.
You passed upon the beach, a dreaming girl,
And clasped a white shell with your flying feet;
The shrouded breezes took you out to sea.
So proud and secret glitters now the pearl
Where sea and sky and thought have come to rest,
And it lies far off and enriches me.

'Waiting for Bayley'

Waiting for Bayley I remark
The ink deserted in the pot
And papers lying in a stark
Abandonment where John is not.

The clock is ticking silently –
Not that I am too deaf to hear,
But since it makes no melody
Of noise except when John is near.

It's also very cold because
I don't know how to light the fire,
(Or don't attempt to diagnose
The tricky gadgets of my dear.)

Abrupted at this point by John
I had to set aside this task,
Explain my sad depression
And all his consolation ask.

What had this gentle sage to say
But 'eat a biscuit, drink some wine!'
The cosmic sorrows of the day
Must all pretention resign.

With laughter and with love beset
And drunk with burgundy and you
I will embrace you and forget
That grief as well as love is true.

Poem for A, who asked for one when I was feeling uninspired

(Arnaldo Momigliano)

And if you think you can command the Muse
And make her come so far in so much rain
To help you write a sonnet, ode, or blues
I'm much afraid you'll have to think again.

This is the season when the Muse is off,
And with her sisters in a rocky hall
Underneath Helicon, she sits to quaff,
Playing at cards, ambrosial alcohol.

So you may ring the bell until you bust
She has her rights, altho' she knows her place;
With the severe detachment of the just
She calmly drops a trump upon an ace.

So you must rattle up your words like bones
To write a poem for that wretched man,
And toss the dried up epithets like stones
Into the literary frying pan,

Hoping that if you make sufficient din
The absent one will turn up after all
Anxious to see what sort of tale you spin
And why you've now decided not to call.

But this device is plainly off the mark;
The moon is hidden in a gloomy haze,
And there's no figure coming through the dark
To set the later stanzas in a blaze.

And so to him this sorry poem limps,
Written with loving thoughts but not with art –
Hoping that in between the lines he'll glimpse
The tenderness of a familiar heart.

Advice to Young Girls

Now lead me and read me
The fables that sadly
Describe how the deeds we
Perform may end badly.
Girls that got mixed up
With gods in the story
So rarely got fixed up
Or settled in glory.
Soft feathers you feel
And the shagginess stroke,
They are armoured with steel
For the flesh they provoke.
Just take it from me, dear,
In labour you'll greet so
For the savour of fear
And the hours that you fleet so
In rivery reed-beds
Embracing and lacing
With bodies whose heads
You would perish in facing.
How much you'll be wishing
You'd lain with another
When monsters come pushing
To call you their mother!
For mortals are dull
But you know where you are,
Nor find yourself full
Of a bird or a star.

Let gods with sad faces
Go past in their legion
At last to their places
In some distant region,
Passing, and touching
And failing to meet,
While cattle come rushing
And licking their feet –
You do not be shaken
By brown eyes of sorrow;
Your day will be taken
But on your tomorrow
You'll lie in the cover
With nothing to light you
And beasts crawling over
Your body will bite you.
So don't be took in
By the beating of wings,
Just turn to your man,
And attend to your things.
Don't walk by the mead
On your way back from shopping:
The trees taking heed
And the singing birds stopping.
The noise in the woodland
Is music of flutes
And under the good land
It's shaking the roots.
But come by the road,
By the five o'clock tram,

And reach your abode
Before evening grows strong.
The gentle recalling
Of fur and of feather
Will wait till you're falling
To slumber together.

Musical Evening for Three

(Philippa and Michael Foot)

Out of my heart the hurricane blows forth
That I had thought forever held in check
By mountainous rocks of time, and that dull earth
That blocks the entrance of the soul, and thick
Collects to barricade us from the North.
I am again the scattering and the wreck
That once I was – and the return of day
Will find my wreckage on what was my way.

I had not thought such pain were possible
Again, not that particular pain.
It is the echo that is terrible –
To find one's spirit can be bent again
Into that old and agonising spiral,
To taste upon the lips the very shame,
Tasted again like wine brought from its rest
To shake the memory of an aged guest.

It was the music that destroyed my peace –
And then that you, and you, were present too.
I could have borne it in another place,
Or, without that assault, encountered you.
But such a power the melody to pierce
My spirit had – the intricate and true
Pattern of all I lived and was, was there
And hung between us trembling in the air.

And then I could no more restrain my tears,
And you, and you, could not restrain your eyes,
And frozen still we sat as if our ears
Could save us from the shattering of surprise –
And still the music played. A thousand spears
In fierce facades of accusation rise,
Uplifted in an agony of sound
To make me cast myself upon the ground.

As so I did, and so you saw me do,
Though others there observed no thing at all,
Except the music could affect me so –
Until to save myself I tried to call
On some strange laughter that is always new
Where pain is always old. The blows that fall
Fall always where the wound is – but the cry
Of joy can make fresh earth and a fresh sky.

I tried to laugh – but memory absolute
Still kept me wailing in the ancient showers.
So many years since you, and you, were hurt
By sins of mine and I by joys of yours.
All this I had imagined was bound up
And purged away by many humble hours
When I had lain amid the visible wreck
And felt the weight relentless on my neck.

But now with terrible precision those
Things that we did together to all three
Appear like visions – and the music flows
Into the tempest of our reverie.
Or do I dream that you too can compose
As well as I that bitter symphony?
Your smiling at each other makes me doubt –
Perhaps in this thing too you leave me out.

The music ends. Politeness does not fail.
I and the others say that we must go.
The door has opened on the evening pale,
The door has opened and I must go through.
The mountains close on the tormenting gale.
What did the music say to you, and you?
The structure of the past remains intact.
I weep for love, impaled upon the fact.

To B, who brought me two candles as a present

(Brigid Brophy)

You brought to me twin lights to symbolise
What? In the complication of your heart
You have me bound with the turning of your eyes,
But to undo me with perpetual art.
How patiently the candle flames endure
That by your bed unvacillating gleam
Through all our talk of sickness and of cure,
Steadily bright till quenched in their own stream.
What you require of me no science gives –
To make these fires constant but not consumed.
What blazes every moment when it lives
Has eaten its own substance as it bloomed.
Yet though they burn not all the evening through,
While they are burning each to each is true.

For B, who tried to persuade me of something in a somewhat Freudian metaphysical poem

(Brigid Brophy)

Thanks for your poem (Freudian) received.
I must confess I found it quite a tonic,
And hope you will not be unduly peeved
If I reply in spirit more ironic.
I doubt in fact if you will be aggrieved
At being greeted in a style Byronic,
Since mixing of the sexes, which you prize,
Lord Byron certainly exemplifies.

How cleverly you write! It's quite confusing.
You want me female, then you want me male,
Or else hermaphrodite, to suit your choosing,
While for yourself you have some other tale
Of corresponding moves. (You *are* amusing!)
To understand this stuff I simply fail,
Eschewing Freud and all his patter, for I
Don't make of sex a basic category.

Of course one *has* a sex, I can't deny it.
For purposes of passports, clothes etcetera
I am a woman, and I don't decry it.
Since man has always done his best to fetter her
A woman would be man, if she could try it,
In many cases; but this would not better her
In any deep respect, and as a spirit
Woman is man's superior in merit.

But I digress. Now turning from page one
I see you speak of locks where keys can go.
It's *most* obscure, and I suspect a *pun*,
Or some obscene and nasty *jeu de mots*;
And how can we be lock and key in one
And also wax? It's hardly *comme il faut*
To make your metaphor quite so inflated
Even when urging something complicated.

And then this talk of *lying*. No, my dear,
Since something to your purpose in me lacks –
Or rather, something *not* so (am I clear?)
I will be neither lock nor key nor wax:
Not closed, yet not for lying on, I fear,
(Or lying *with*. You make us sound like sacks!)
Nor by such entry to be prised apart
As rudely searching would not move my heart.

But why should I spend time to tell you this?
Your own ingenious spirit needs no lesson.
Nature denies us a consummate bliss
But gives us much to rest our happiness on.
Too great exactitude would come amiss.
Half sundered and in darkness we must press on.
For what it darkly is, then take my love
And in the forest lost we still shall rove.

Conversations with a Prince c. 1963

1
Declaration

2
Encounter

3
Absence

4
Conversations with a Prince

5
Remembrance

Declaration

Reading of Palms

(with Julian Chrysostomides)

There is a spirit that has come to fly
About among the glasses and the plates.
You open my hand and peruse the fates
Sorting the ribbons of their mystery.
Unspoken love has made us discontent.
You read a poem in another tongue.
The wine is finished and the candle spent.
Unspoken love has made me stay too long.
Trace out that gentle monogram aright
Where chance and nature wrote me down my part
Of being yours but too discreetly so.
Make us the conscious sovereigns of delight.
Retain my hand and look into my heart,
You who love me and do not know I know.

Refusal to Sing

(with Julian Chrysostomides)

Now you are angry, or pretend to be,
Because I say I will not sing a song.
We are a little drunk with poetry,
Claret, and flowers of summer, and the long
Discreet endurance of a conversation
Wherein we are as snakes that intertwine;
We complicate the knot of our relation
To incarnate an unforeseen design.
Tonight we spoke of everything but love.
We who have come in company so far
Affect to be unconscious how we move.
Your hand is still as distant as a star.
I write this incantation in lieu
Of what I dare not utter without words.
This is the song that I withheld from you.
Morning besieges us with many birds
And still our moments break that cannot hold
The overflowing content of the heart.
We laugh, being unable to enfold
The awkwardness that keeps us still apart.

Word Watcher

(for John Bayley)

Watching the words that come and go
In arcs conjectured but not seen,
Mere flashes in the foliage,
I think of you, and thinking so
Conjure the deep and flickering green
To sharpen for me its mirage.

Too speedy for the sight to catch,
The cantering horse through centuries
The movement of its limbs concealed
From human eyes too gross to match
The structure of those mysteries
To cameras alone revealed.

Yet intricate philosophy
Had words for servants too, and they
Were these same words that wildly flew
Coloured with speed invisibly,
And yet were tame enough to say
The things that Kant and Plato knew.

Deep in the wood I lie apart,
And know of words only the cries
And see the blur and not the wing,
And carry in my loaded heart
What makes it founder with its prize,
Divided from the word, the thing.

Oh populated woodland where
The treetops with the clouds converse
And leaves to other leaves can come
And voice with other voices share
In speech that echoes will disperse
And only what is dead is dumb –

Be still for me, dear sounds, and tell
The truth which in the roundelay
Laments the pain of scattering.
You can be steadfast if you will;
Pause now, and let your silence say
What caught would be compelled to sing.

Forest Fire

(with Julian Chrysostomides)

These are not the proper words
Nor is this communication.
From the burning wood the birds
Fly in fear of conflagration.

On the earth the leafy blaze
Kills whatever cannot rise,
Suffocating clouds will craze
What must burn before it dies.

Beating wings within the smoke,
You will spread yourselves in vain,
Try to speak and only choke,
Long for miracles of rain.

In the dreadful night they crash
That were once so tall and gay,
And tomorrow brings the ash
And the blackened spears of day.

In this darkness of our fears
Hear a melody of birds.
Water with repentant tears
This our foliage of words.

'How far is the green cliff'

(with Arnaldo Momigliano in a tea shop)

How far is the green cliff across the still
Water reflecting in a towery haze
The pine trees and the solemn skies that fall
Into the quiet ocean of our days?
The boat that takes us to it hardly moves
Anchored into its image in the glass,
And locked in sun and silence our two loves
Wait for the storm and are afraid to pass.
But take your glance from the horizon's line
And study through the water's polished floor
The population of the tranquil sea.
We need not wait to see the god's design;
There is no riddle hidden on the shore,
We are already deep in what will be.

Pine Branches

(for John Bayley)

Where the pine tree bough is broken
There I see our world in little,
Bringing needles that are brittle,
Sharp and brittle, for a token.
Pine boughs for a gift I brought,
Damp with resin, dry with cones,
Rustling like rising bones
In a wind of judgment caught.
These are murmuring and swaying
Pine trees in the tempest's strife
Near the places where my knife
Took the parting from the staying.
These are dusty, grey, and dying,
Severed from the tossing heads.
Puzzled in our separate beds
We are broken off and lying.
Reach toward me in the night,
Snap the branches with your hand,
Perfume of a southern land
Will be with you till the light.

The Shell (2)

(with Julian Chrysostomides)

These coupled domes of shadow are concealing
The enclosed perfume of a long summer of birds,
Resonant dully like the sea, revealing
What was not told in all our noon of words.
Your darkness now holds all the soft suspended
Particles of that green and sunny dell,
Retained within the tenderly tense extended
Wings of a wave-washed bone-white ocean shell.
Shadows and shells curve with the ever-breaking
Time that we cannot resist, whose rhythm scatters
Designs that were once our days, and the rainbow tinge
Of our former conversation at last is taking
The foam of another tide; but all that matters
Is held by that curling relentlessly tender hinge.

Encounter

Picture on a Tablecloth

(for John Bayley)

All art aspires to music, so they say,
But this to be a painting rather yearns;
And you, the judge of this obscure essay
Will know the flame originally burns
In the diffusion of an evening mood
Where you and winter are dissolved in wine
And satisfied with speech and full of food
I want to make the moment still more mine.
So let me draw across the sleepy scene
The formal pattern of poetic thought,
So that we may reflect on what has been
And even catch the whisper of what ought.
You, my companion of so many hours
Spent walking barefoot in the breaking wave
Or in the silver curtains of the showers
Where mountain-tops prostrate themselves to pave
The way that leads to where the river flows
That legend says destroys the memory,
To where above our heads the branches close –
Repeat with me this murmurous litany.
Bright in the branches still the birds are seen –
And after all the picture into song
Is changing and the disappearing green
Makes music for us all the evening long.
Colour is silent and the night is come
And only voices linger overhead.
When all the daylight animals are dumb
The tongues of nightingales shall carve our bed.

Oxford to Paddington

(for John Bayley)

The rail strike made the station desolate.
You came to see me off with chocolate
And celebration of your candid eyes
Which always look upon me with surprise
And tenderness and questioning and fear,
Like to the hesitation of a deer
All poised and trembling between flight and love:
A simile which doubtless will not move
You much, except perhaps to irritation.
The train appeared at last and left the station
About the time predicted by the guard,
And now I'm travelling and trying hard
To write a poem at sixty miles per hour.
Out of the window I can see a flower,
Or flowers rather, but I have to rhyme,
Which I would pick for you if there was time.
The white hawthorn is out and through the green
Of all the hedges spreads its dewy cream,
And buttercups are very shiny too,
And here and there I apprehend a blue
Sense datum, which I rather think denotes
Material presence of forget-me-nots.
The towers of Oxford fall beneath the brow
And I am wondering if you are now
In the Bodleian working hard perhaps,
Or drinking Spanish sherry with some chaps.
In this tempestuous life how little chance
We have to meditate on Providence

That sets these unsought passions in the soul,
And makes the wave-bestriding spirit roll
Like a corvette in the Ionian sea.
The gentle force that circles you and me
Is tender as the murmur of the south,
And yet as all-compelling as the north,
Or that great power without which, says Hume,
Our minds would perish quite and go to ruin.
I am a peril to your inmost heart
Which is divided by that famous dart,
So that with blood in furious insurrection
It lies an open wound to all infection.
The little that I have is poor indeed,
I am made wealthy only by your need.
If many others in my life have place
How can I bear to look into your face
Who make such total warfare of your love?
Precarious the sphere in which we move,
And yet I could believe it without ending,
Fixed by a miracle of understanding.
I'll study in the book of constancy
And pray you hold me in your clemency.
The grace in you must be enough for both
And make my stammering a kind of truth.
So kiss me now and take my soul in keeping.
I shall spend the rest of the journey sleeping,
Or feigning to, since further song is vain,
A man from Porlock having joined the train.

Ravenna

(for Arnaldo Dante Momigliano)

In the sun descending upon an Italian city
Pallid on pillars in gold and red upon crenellations,
We seek for the vestiges of ancient terror and pity
And see from the café table the tide of civilisations.

Near to the tomb of Dante walking towards the evening
You told me how Italy's heart here in Ravenna began
To beat, and out of the barbarous empire streaming
Into a scintillation of golden mosaic ran.

You, walking and bowing your head in the square of San Francesco,
How present you are to all of the city's modern heart;
Or, head thrown back, you are immobile contemplating a fresco,
Splendidly gentle when thus you are set by yourself apart.

You with the name you bear, the name of the poet that's sleeping –
Exiled like you, he learnt the love of a distant place –
Turning over the thoughts in your scholar's heart, and keeping
The painfully complex past present before your face,

Wait for me still a while in the San Francesco piazza
And read in the patient book that lives in your pocket always,
And do not tire of telling this ignorant ragazza
What it was like long ago in the Greek and Roman days.

'The sun has left the garden'

(with Arnaldo Momigliano)

The sun has left the garden and the rain
Falls with the leaves from summer-weary trees.
The cuckoo hesitates, falls silent, flees,
And heaven blackens with a running stain.
We turn from watching at the window and
Are caught by looking in each other's eyes.
We see the terror of the storm's surprise
And heavy breakers on a rainy sand.
But this in summer is a single day
And this in years a single season is,
When earth is muddy and when rain is cold.
I touch you as you turn to go away,
And see the lightning flash of happiness
Even in consciousness of growing old.

Winter Snapshot

I hold a snapshot of you in my hand,
A years-old one I took when once the park
Was flooded. You remember? There you stand
Hands deep in pockets in the gathering dark
Of hollow tawny misty winter air
And water at your feet where meadows were.

Everyone was excited by the flood.
We came each day to see the waters rise.
Such harmless violence beguiled our mood
Who were in train for true catastrophes,
Or so we thought. Image of human ill,
Sheets of relentless water rising still.

The golden reeds are foundered in the tide,
Half way up willows mounts the chuckling surge.
Bewildered swans and drunken mallards ride
To distances where mist and water merge,
And momentary winter sunshines bring
Us rosy branches innocent of spring.

Blurred as a Chinese print, in that pale day
You on the water sailing sorrow too
As if the flood were taking you away
And what we feared of parting were come true.
I show this picture to you to remind
Of fears our love triumphant left behind.

Absence

You by Telephone

Murmuring to my dear with telephonic assistance
How like a top my heart circles in wild gyration!
Thanks to modern science love can speak at a distance
And absences are riddled with possible conversation;
So now at any moment as I sit by my fireside musing,
Nursing the bruises I got from careless Cupid's rod,
I can conjure up the voice that is sovereign of my choosing,
That utters from afar the oracle of the god.
Such is the music that waits if I care to lift the receiver:
Luckier I than those severed in ancient days,
Who could not talk to the girl after they had to leave her;
No wonder constancy wasn't one of their traits,
In spite of the case of Odysseus, who might have got home much
     sooner
If at the start he could have dialled Ithaca one.
But he might have offended Hermes, that rival tele-communer,
And science would have precluded a lot of Homer's fun.
Now to return to you, my dear, that I hold at the end of
The wire, as Ariadne held her lover by art,
The truth is I am afraid of exercising this brand of
Magic to bring you nearer, you who live in my heart.
Talking belongs with loving, and speech is a lover's keeper;
Yet what a piercing wound a thoughtless word can give,
And your words without your eyes, my darling, can cut me deeper
When I cannot see the head where my hazard fortunes live.
And I hear your voice in the dark, and my yearning spirit staggers,
I seek for words myself and cannot understand,

For I cannot close with kisses the lips that may speak me daggers,
Nor give you a gentle answer just by taking your hand.
I can see the point of Propertius' desire for perpetual fighting,
Nam sine amore gravi femina nulla dolet,
But I prefer to see the person I'm kicking and biting
When I am in the arena whose bounds by Love are set.
So forgive me if I am silent and do not constantly ring you,
Though in my heart I never cease to call your name,
And let these foolish verses untelephonically bring you
The old news of a love that steadily stays the same.

Conversations with a Prince

I Overcome Love

Love threw me to the ground in equal fight
And, laughing, with his knee upon my chest
Asked me what I proposed to do. The light
Burnt in his eyes from vigour of contest
And wide he spread his wings but not for flight.
I, feigning weakness, to contrive a rest
Began to reason with him, and he bent
Over me close, eager for argument.

'What pride is there', I asked, 'in quick defeat?
You had the better of me here, it's true –
But the ground was uneven, and my feet
Struck on a stone. An expert such as you
Knows well when it is chance and strength that meet
Not strength and strength. Dear me, I've lost a shoe!'
I hoped at this he would relax his hold,
But still he held me down. The ground was cold.

'Come, come,' said Love, 'in your philosophy
You like to argue that a human's power
Is measured by his deeds, not secretly
Concealed in faculties that never flower
In open skill. Not accidentally,
My dear, its mine to crow and yours to cower!
Those who are weak are those who come to harm.'
At this point he began to twist my arm.

I was in pain. 'I grant it then,' I said,
'You are the stronger, I am overthrown.
It would be scandal if a heavenly god
Had not the power to hurl a mortal down.
The vision of defeat was in my head
Before our bodies touched – and like a stone
I tumbled at the terror of your grip.'
I stopped a wail by savaging my lip.

'You shift your ground!' said Love – and radiance
Shone from his sovereign face. 'You argue now
From destiny and not from evil chance.
But many mortals, as you surely know',
(I tried to turn my head to shun his glance,
So full of scorn it was), 'give blow for blow,
And drive me out!' He underlined his quip,
Clapping a wing like cracking of a whip.

'Though Dido fell, Aeneas did not stay',
Said Love, quite moved, 'upon the Tyrian shore;
And even Dido's face faded away.
He did not recognise her any more,
Though Virgil did not say so, on the day
They met in Hades. He did not explore
The faces of the dead that in a ring
Surrounded him for any passionate thing.

'And I could mention others' – 'No!' I said,
'In strife with you another's fate is naught.
I am not moved by the illustrious dead,
The net where the consenting heart is caught
Is of its own devising, rarely made.
This, the particular agony I sought
Is mine to wear. If I exist at all
I am this pain, this struggle and this fall.'

Love was triumphant and he arched upon
Me like an eagle pinning to his prey,
And shook me, and his flaming tresses spun
Like lightning in my backward turning eye.
My throat was white and stretched. His beauty shone
Like comets raining down continually.
With bones and blood in fatal insurrection
I saw the last things and my own destruction.

I cried out hardly knowing what I cried.
Some last preserving instinct gave me grace.
'You said that you were Love, but how you lied!
I know your real name!' His strong embrace
Was loosened suddenly, and terrified
The god and I were kneeling face to face.
Like animals for slaughter in one tether
Huddled and shivering we clung together.

Overheard

I called to Love in the darkness of the evening,
Calling quietly, afraid of waking someone
Who slept beside me. Radiant and pale
As a glow-worm through the thorny branches
Of the twining net-work of the rose-bower looking
The face of Love was lifted above me
And I spoke to him trembling in the danger of his presence,
Asking and beseeching him to find me a solution.
Love was very gentle with me that evening.
He understood my grief but could not find me a solution.
So for an hour we talked together in low voices
Very close to each other through the leafy lattice
And with the warm night air I breathed the perfume
Of his divine proximity. He left me
At last, and the pale glow in the garden faded
That had seemed like moonlight, and I moved from the place
Where behind the pattern of flowers I had been kneeling;
And saw in the heavy darkness behind me
Gleaming the wide-open eyes of a listener.

Love Keeps the Maze

I try to thread the labyrinth, but beat
As I may about to foil the old design
I am the slave of monotonous feet
Following the same pattern every time.
Hope still persuades me that I may undo
This knotted grief. And so I run until
The old old barriers arise anew
And fence me from the heart of my own will.
High in the maze's centre on a ladder
Sits Love the keeper watching through the green
Walls my poor wandering, and holding back
The shout that could direct me. Which is madder,
The god who has invented this machine
Or I who see his face but not the track?

I Seek for Love at the Carnaval

The evening of the carnaval was warm,
Lights in the garden cunningly displayed,
While under swinging lamps the masquerade
Tangled in streamers rages like a storm.
I sought my lord deep in the coloured fray.
Not hard to find: he could not mask his eyes;
And in his chequered arms till the sunrise
I danced, and talked my troubles all away.
In chilly daylight for my cloak I ask
And through the small rain walk towards my home,
Wondering suddenly if it was he.
Throughout the night he did not leave his mask.
Have I unloaded so my heart to one
Who was not Love but only seemed to be?

Love Makes my Heart a Shrine

Coiled black and glittering Love at his ease
Watches me, while I cry, 'Not this again,
Shot through the body, quaking at the knees,
Made void with longing and filled up with pain,
Fixed with most violent and *intransigeant* will
Upon another I cannot possess:
Make passion poison in my blood until
I die for him, let that be happiness!'
Love answered, 'There will be no end of weeping –
Oceans of tears will make your wounds to grow
Until the parting flesh lays the heart bare.
Your conscious senses still their vigil keeping
In contemplation, though the flesh cries no,
Will keep him burning to my glory there.'

Love Visits his Traps

Love going round his traps to see what gain
The night had brought, discovered me once more
Ensnared in the same place; and with a roar,
Grounding his shot-gun, laughed, 'What, you again?
You were so wounded last time and so sick,
When I released you, you were almost dead!'
I lay in bracken and my blood and said,
'My Lord, you have a gun, despatch me quick.'
He knelt beside me in the mist, and where
The steel had bitten to the very bone
He laid his hand until the pain had ceased.
I slept, and dreamed that distant was made near,
And cruel kind. Pain wakened me at noon,
Horribly wounded but again released.

Love Solves a Problem for Me

Stark mad at a crossroads I stood and found
That either road was death, yet one must be
Taken. My open mouth with agony
In wailing of my fate was red and round.
Where the two roads divided like a stone
I lay, until I heard a distant horse,
And saw my master come in violent course
Toward me till he almost rode me down.
I lifted to my knees and cried, 'No more!
I can endure no more, let me go back!'
Love raised his whip and cleft me at a blow,
Then jerked me upright spitted to the core,
And forced me to go onward. Down each track
Maimed and divided now I weeping go.

I Attempt Escape

I reached the frontier at dead of night.
The stream was pale where my steps had to go.
I paused to listen. Forest and shadow
In vegetable silence kept my flight.
Cool water takes my ankle and my knee.
Disturbing stars I pass the narrow bed.
Now golden-footed on the fields I tread
The mounting measure of my liberty.
As tall as Satan in my way he stands,
His arc of wings unfolding, as I scream,
'I've left the country you are master of!'
I turn and run for terror of his hands,
And as I stumble back across the stream
I hear the thunderous mockery of Love.

I See Love in Bad Company

The night with sheets of vaporous rain was cloaked.
The moon was carrying a little cloud.
At the street corner I perceived a crowd
Of young and slender dandies who provoked
The passers-by. I hurried past the place,
Anxious for home – but in the lamp-light saw
Amid that grouped impertinent guffaw
Of leering ruffians, a familiar face.
Surely the one that whistles after me
None other is than Love, who did me harm,
Though he was my friend once. Without surprise
I see him now in evil company.
A wicked face – but oh those eyes could charm –
Heart, sudden heart, don't beat me to my knees.

Love Sights a Wreck

I struggled in the wave, Love flew above,
I gasped in the green salt while Love was free.
The crash that let the ocean in on me
Was noticed from afar by cruising Love.
Weaker and weaker through the raging night
I climb the mountains of the violent sea,
Until my wailing mouth is stopped with spray.
Love circles calmly, keeping me in sight.
'Lift me,' I cry, 'you who can always win!
No wreck too terrible for you to salvage.'
'I cannot lift,' said Love, 'from so far down.'
I catch his foot and drag him fluttering in.
Wide scattered on the surge his broken plumage.
I clutch his body laughing and I drown.

I am Consoled by Love

In a city revisited after many years
I heard a voice that called me by my name
In a familiar tone. I paused and came
Into a dark place where to hide my tears.
The atmosphere was strange yet not unknown:
It was a bar crowded with those exiled
And wandering like myself. 'Come here, my child,'
Said Love. 'How nice to see you here alone.
Who shall be host this time, or shall we toss?'
He put his arm around me. Providence
Provides extremity of grief with due
Drugs to obliterate the pain of loss.
'Alone!' I said, 'My Lord, it is no chance.
Deprived of him I find myself with you.'

I Meet an Old Friend

I met with Love, my former friend,
And idly talked the hour through,
Remembering people that we knew
Together once, and at the end
I rose to go, distressed to see
How ill he looked and how dejected,
And knew in that ruined face reflected
How these same years had altered me.
'Tomorrow let us meet. Who knows – ?'
Said Love. 'I am not free', I said –
But soon forgot that I was wise
Again, again bewitched by those,
Still brilliant in the ageing head,
Commanding and familiar eyes.

I Encounter my Old Master

I stood once at a cross-roads wondering
Which way to take; it was an autumn day.
A figure with a broom was labouring,
Collecting leaves: but as he swept away
The ones upon the road he was deceived
By the fierce wind that would not let him gain,
And ever at his back the golden-leaved
Forest was falling in continual rain.
I idly watched a while. Then suddenly
I recognised the creature. It was Love,
My former Master, in a ragged guise.
I spoke to him most courteously – but he
Seemed not to hear. The rising tempest drove
Torrents of leaves into his crazy eyes.

Love Brought Down

The path was clipped and smooth between
The hazy walls of summer grass.
Walking with you I made to pass,
But saw that something in the green
Lay fallen. One enormous wing
Had spread the field with ragged silk.
How long he lay and pale as milk
Amid the broken feathering.
His eyes were witless in his head.
I stroked his body without fear
Beneath the softly plumaged vault.
You came and asked me, 'Is Love dead?'
I wept and answered, 'No, my dear,
But maimed and maddened through my fault.'

Love Smiles upon Us

(for John Bayley)

Out with my dear on February nights
We found the cloven frost-embittered earth,
Bedraggled with old leaves, had given birth
To small bright golden stemless aconites.
So at our feet those echoes of the sky
And, gazing at each other, heaven too
Equally mirrored, when we were aware
Of one who smiled upon us and passed by.
I knew, before you asked, the stranger's name,
Whose radiance grew behind you like a flower,
For it was he who once with grievous rod
Made all my woe in years before you came,
Yet brought me still his pilgrim to this hour.
I answered, 'It is Love, a gentle god.'

Remembrance

A Fallen Tree in the University Parks

(for Julian Chrysostomides)

You asked me to come and see a fallen tree
And on the way towards it you were sad
Because you thought I might be disappointed.
It was near evening and obscurity
Lay brown and hazy on the path that led
Across the river to the place appointed.
Then when we reached the bridge we found the gate
Was locked, and I could see you hesitate.

Already you were traitor to your tree
And ready to go home. I set my foot
Before discussion started, on the rail.
We climbed the gate with no more ceremony.
You walked ahead of me, prepared to put
Your heart into the water, where the pale
Last gold of evening lingered in the ditch
Under the willow tree to make us rich.

Your tree lay down – and its long fingers stretched
A little distance through the rising meadow,
Its roots grotesque with hanging earth and bare.
A melancholy stole from it and reached
Us like a mist, and standing in the shadow
Of other trees that merged into the air
We shivered, and returning through the park
We heard the dead leaves rustling in the dark.

We felt the particles of darkness freeze
And pierce the hollow gold of evening through.
The light was faded even from the stream.
We ran in silence through the watching trees
To reach the other gate, before it too
Was shut upon us – and we saw the gleam
Of lamplight and the headlights of the cars,
While all the Park was looking at the stars.

And you were silent still because you thought
I had been disappointed in your tree,
And I was silent, being too much moved.
And somehow you had lost the thing you sought
In trying to discover it to me –
And quietly you mourned for what you loved.
We were sad then and had no words at all.
I am sad now for what words can't recall.

Nightingales near the London Road

(for Stella Aldwinckle)

Stopping the car, we heard the nightingale
And climbed the ploughed field from the busy road.
The night was dark and blue and waiting there.
Below us an illuminated trail
Of cars and lorries east and westward flowed
While we went on alone to mount the stair
Of earth toward the voice upon the ridge
Beyond the pallid elder of the hedge.

We reached the top with clay upon our shoes,
Drawn by that pure serrated line of sound.
Before us lay the structure of the wood.
First deep in grass, then walking upon moss
And then on beech leaves seeking a way round
We skirted fences till at last we stood
Close to that cry so piercing and so lonely
Within a cavern made of darkness only.

But that was long ago; and all the joy
Each had of each that led us to that place
Is dead, and we to other loves do turn.
In just such pictures you I still enjoy,
Revisiting your dark and spellbound face.
Let me for you in equal image burn.
When detailed memory of our passion fails
We'll meet each other with the nightingales.

Snowdrops

Earliest forms upstarting purely from
Bedraggled earth of winter's disarray
You little pale as marble snowdrops come,
White flowers, children of a white day.
Muffled and muted is the word you bring,
Unconscious dreamers of uncertain spring.

An ancient temple by a southern sea
Built by the godlike Greeks in a lost time
Crumbles to pieces which attentively
The green transparent water will refine
To polished pebbles in its glass to keep:
Such perfect tears the kneeling ages weep.

My marble teardrops snowdrops let me share
The loneliness of your attention
Under a pale pavilion of cold air
As white as truth and empty of the sun:
A bitter hope is best that makes to grow
White thoughts of spring that only winter know.

The past made perfect and the future blind
In a still moment of the year's midnight,
Humble device of an expectant mind
Fingered by time to unconsoling light,
Our sober knowledge that the earth must run
To lean into the bosom of the sun.

Poems 1972–1995

Colour Patches

A warm and sopping autumn day
With the bemused birds singing as if it were spring
Brings gentle and precise thoughts, these
Vivid fragments all our certainty
When leafless spears of pale mauve crocuses
Pierce wet and draggled grass
And orange roses glow in morning haze
After the swallows go,
And birds that bide are more domestic with us.
Coppery rhus and bright catalpa glow
And green woodpeckers laugh in powdery light
In mist-burned afternoons scooped by the sun
Into great fiery chasms of bright leaves.
Collared dove grieves
And tumbles in the haze
In murmurous hushes
Into pale yellow ivy bushes.

Transparent autumn crocus
And hollow pigeon's cry
Make the world sink into obscurity.
Sweet that vague sense of wisdom on the tongue.
Honeyed false insights, huge tasks undone.
Dear inward garden be
In spite of all disintegration
All that is misty and without sense,
A place of mercy and reconciliation
And some obstinate innocence

Where quiet roses make the time
A celebration of simplicity
Dew that the sun
Even in hours of shining cannot drink.
Unbind the bandage of anxiety
And let some silent ray unseal
The empty hollow places where we feel and think.

Child Prays

A child learning to pray
Said to God as if He was there.
No manifestation, nothing on fire,
Not an uneasy cranny anywhere,
So must the world be rent?

As the archangel appeared
Meek Mary once
Sitting in a shed
Fell about seared
While wooden slats were dropping everywhere

For a split second the universe rattled
Every atom glowed pure white.
Something *did* happen.
(A spatio-temporal continuum
Has its own kind of event.)

Must God be burning so?
Gathers it with the rest,
And what's more he's right,
The child learning.
That holocaust? Mere art work. Goodnight.

No third degree burns after all
Not even lurid, nothing perished.
Wooden and rather small instead,
Among small and cherished
Things. God cat and dog and bed.

Odysseus on Calypso's Island

A harbour. A place of lanterns seen in a dream.
There are places for us and other places
Which are utterly ours and yet nowhere.
Scatteredness is our way
But still we dream of home,
Home is a deep idea,
That we are home and one.
Seas drown us, roads divide us so,
And still we ride, still, still we go.

Broken our ways, blunted
The intent of a returning.
Once on an island I wondered
If I had merely dreamed of a place
That haunted me in my sleep, or whether
It really existed, and that so plucked me, pulled me.
The lights lit, the dog barking,
A recognition. Remembering then an embrace.
A face haunts my dreams.
Yet living here has its loveliness
Nevertheless, and I do live here.

The sea is a problem.
That line, how can I question it,
How really understand it, unravel its mystery?
I long for an authority in my life.
But surely the authorities were burnt.
I saw them burn, indeed
I made them burn.

The long ago
Puzzles my tired mind.
A purpose was achieved.
A great aim of destruction
So golden in intention, what became
Of all that splendour?
I can only remember clearly
A bleeding man dead in much trampled mud.
And a wounded horse.

I am tired, perhaps I am drugged,
Perhaps she drugs me.
We get blind drunk together every evening.

Some self-styled tavern sage
Said once that they were one.
A woman is always the same,
He said, wherever you find her, one and eternal.
I ask the sea's line if this is true.
The sea disturbs me. Once
I started to make a boat.
I left it on the stones and the sea took it away
Mocking – but with what meaning?

I wonder if faithfulness is
Any thing. A concept certainly.
To do with that long horizontal line
With which I live, with which I have always
Lived. Never out of sight of the sea,
Never, my boy, be out of sight of the sea.
My father said once some place.

Sometimes I just relax and dream.
To spend days simply lying in the sun
That, on a windy plain once,
I dreamed of as paradise,
To rest the body. To be clean,
To lie in a bed, to lie in a garden,
To be without fear of death.
I remember how tired I was all the time.
Days and days when we did not disarm.
Was it worth it? Was that worth that?
A very beautiful woman
And a sound foreign policy.
I cannot properly remember either.
A foreign policy, a lovely girl.

Sleeping or waking not sure,
Lying on the shore in the heat
Of the noon which silences the birds,
Silences even cicadas,
Lying in a sticky swell of pines

Crackling the splintered sun with dazed eyes,
Dozing I see a woman's face with sudden clarity.
Not very beautiful perhaps but full of meaning
And an assembled place, and
A thought of returning.
Do her eyes accuse me?

At night in her embrace
When we have drunk ourselves to sleep and joy
I live the present in a real love.
I live here after all
Give me the cup, I will drink your potion
Whatever it contains. Drink it all up.
Take me in your arms, present
Beauty beyond compare,
Beauty of the gods
Untroubling and rare. Hold me,
Enfold me in my only here.
Take away fear of a returning.
A city burning is not upon my soul.
It was not my idea, never my plan, intention.

I anticipated something successful and brief,
Not all that blood and all those years,
Not all those tears, tears.
I did not foresee such an absence.
Hold me and bury my head
In a darkness that glows slow and red.

Only at dawn it troubles me
Silver or grey the horizon
The hard line of the sea
Something disturbs me deeply then.
My head aches. Tears come then, tears that are like bleeding.
'Where have you gone? Do not always sit there on the shore.
Come home my darling.'
Between leaves speeding the radiant goddess.

So kind to me, what could be kinder, what
Greater bliss than to live ever thus?

She tells the mist to take away
The torment of the sea, removes
It from me for another day, so surely she
Is home and love?
Give me the cup, the cup.

John Sees a Stork at Zamora

Walking among quiet people out from mass
He saw a sudden stork
Fly, from its nest upon a house.
So blue the sky, the bird so white,
For all these people an accustomed sight.

He took his hat off in sheer surprise
And stood and threw his arms out wide
Letting the people pass
Him by on either side
Aware of nothing but the stork-arise.

On a black tapestry now
This gesture of joy
So absolutely you.

Agamemnon Class 1939

(In Memoriam Frank Thompson 1920–1944)

Do you remember Professor
Eduard Fraenkel's endless
Class on the *Agamemnon*?
Between line eighty-three and line a thousand
It seemed to us our innocence
Was lost, our youth laid waste,
In that pellucid unforgiving air,
The aftermath experienced before,
Focused by dread into a lurid flicker,
A most uncanny composite of sun and rain.
Did we expect the war? What did we fear?
First love's incinerating crippling flame,
Or that it would appear
In public that we could not name
The aorist of some familiar verb.
The spirit's failure we knew nothing of,
Nothing really of sin or of pain,
The work of the knife and the axe,
How absolute death is,
Betrayal of lover and friend,
Of egotism the veiled crux,
Mistaking still for guilt
The anxiety of a child.
With exquisite dressage
We ruled a chaste soul.
They had not yet made an end
Of the returning hero.
The demons that travelled with us
Were still smiling in their sleep.

Heralded by the cries of hitherto silent Cassandra
The undulating siren creates in the entrails
And in the heart new structures
Of sensation, the abrupt start
Of war, its smell and sound.
The hours distend with bombs,
The big guns vibrate in the ground.
Frightened men kill by remote control
Or face to face appalled see their enemy fall.
Houses and public buildings with a kind of surprise
Bend their knees and turn into tombs.
Ever so many gentle worlds quietly end.
People sleep in catacombs.
White paths of doomed men
Daily criss-cross in the skies.
The sanctuary is bombed and lies
Open and unmysterious,
A garden of wild flowers.
Something crawls wounded on,
But the Holy One
Having suffered too long
Eventually dies.

Delphi medises and Apollo's face grows dim.
Was there a god there? We never saw him.
A priest was making a political sound.
Fey Helen lost her beauty and her shame,
Went home quite pertly in the end they say,
Piously helped the poor, became
A legend haunting a fought-over ground.
What was it for? Guides tell a garbled tale.

The hero's tomb is a disputed mound.
What really happened on the windy plain?
The young are bored by stories of the war.
And you the other young who stayed there
In the land of the past are courteous and pale,
Aloof, holding your fates.
We have to tell you it was not in vain.
Even grief dates, and even Niobe
At last was fed, and you
Are all pain and yet without pain
As is the way of the dead.

No one can rebuild that town
And the soldier who came home
Has entered the machine of a continued doom.
Only the sky and the sea
Are unpolluted and old
And godless with innocence.
And twilight comes to the chasm
And to the sea's expanse
And the terrible bright Greek air fades away.

Poem and Egg

(for Tambi – James Meary Tambimuttu)

I would like to write a poem like a picture
Portraying something rather dark and big
In an atomic sea of pea-green hue,
Or else a sort of lumpy golden thing
In a dark sea of almost blackened blue
Suggesting I suppose the universe,
Not circular in fact but gently squashed,
Shaped like an orange or untapered egg,
A floating egg lonely as everything.

These ancient forms are really very simple,
And anything that sages have to say
Concerning what they symbolised or meant
Is likely to be rather commonplace.
They can be seen as images of God,
His bland unfeatured face,
Or of the great mama her lovely cunt,
Or lazy absolutes of any kind,
Or chaos pierced by mind,
Or simply seas of colour pierced by shape
Or colour swooning in its own embrace.

A poem cannot be like that however,
Its ambiguity will tend to have a point
Which must be muffled, kept from being clever.
A poem can be never quite so plain,
So all-absorbing like an oval mouth.
It has to play a game to tell the truth,

It is more like a little flame,
Words soaked in petrol burning themselves up.
Before the absolute, a pyre of sense
Asking forgiveness of the cosmic egg
For this impertinence.

The Brown Horse

(for Emma Stone)

We fed the brown horse.
From your flattened palms
Delicately he deigns.
He has such gentle ways, diffidently moves
In the wet grass his spreading hooves,
His big head sways,
His legs are dark with dew.
Oh, that was long ago.

Do you remember how we fed the brown horse long ago?
Your hair mingled with his mane as you embraced him.
You laughed because he snuffled so,
Taking the bread with delicate lips.
Great storms had stroked the trees,
There was a grey sea and ships.
Huge-eyed and kind his head,
Wet and so green the grass,
There where he waited to be fed,
Waiting so patiently for us to pass
Long ago.

Light upon water in a dark place
Pleases the peevish hungry for sense,
We change, we are dispersed, oblivious,
We are made up of accidents.
There is no health in us,
But light nevertheless.

Love comes again, again,
And thus identity;
This at least is the same,
The ebb and flow of the sea,
The sudden shine on the ships
Beyond the kneeling tree.

Parts of the world we
Are the parts of parts. So
There was an island and a child? Of course
That much we know,
Remembering the brown horse,
How we fed him long ago.

Motorist and Dead Bird

He felt or thought he felt the crack,
Saw in his mirror the bird-blotted road,
Cursed the compulsion of going back
To find it glossy, without blood, quite dead.
Pinned to the tarmac in a quick fight,
The wings embattled, the affronted eyes,
A sort of sudden trophy, whose near-flight
Still gibbers in the trees.
Swift memory adept at chance
Advantages implants the sting.
He recalls his wife and how she would have wept
Now, who wept once at such a thing.
She is not dead, not she, nor yet bereft,
But living happily with someone else.
She loved animals. After he left
They said it was a blessing they were childless,
No rancour; she describes her kids in Christmas letters.
He lifts the bird by a long wing-tip up.
Not to feel warm just-fled life is better,
Lays it in the ditch as if that could help,
Where leaves are tender: now abrupts the pains
Of vain remorse; and soon his pale
Headlights will scan the hawthorn lanes
That lead to the obscure hotel
Where he is waited for.
                    He will not tell
His little friend this creepy tale.
Her tears, his spite,
Will end in sleepy night.

Avonmouth Docks

I remember going to Avonmouth docks with my father
When I was a schoolgirl for a summer outing.
I was at a boarding school in Bristol
And we took the train to Avonmouth to see the ships there.
It was a wintry day as I remember and
We wandered among warehouses seeing distant funnels
Then bang! And we saw the men shooting pigeons,
The big grey pigeons were falling on the warehouse roofs
And tumbling down here and there quite near to us
Bang! And the tumbling wings, broken, oh were they still alive.
I was blinded by tears, so sorry
Both for the pigeons and my father
And I knew he grieved for me
Perhaps he was crying too.
He is dead now – I feared his death
Then and I fear it now.

Fox

When coldness blanches the blue sky
And the broken bracken arch
Bends beneath its crystal rind,
Every rifted mound
Cross-gartered golden-browned.
And the earth parched and dry
And the frost is scattered there
Wind-refined in the chill air:
      My footstep creaks in grasses,
      Quietness makes me stare
      While in a woodland space a sudden fox
      Peers with his brilliant face, and passes.

No Smell

A saint upon a mountain stair
Concerned with other things attracted birds
Who roosted there inside his cell.
He all abstract in prayer, his evening candle
Kindled a set of sleepy jewel eyes.
It was the scent of goodness cast the spell
Which simply ceased one day when he
At last enlightened came to be
A perfect man without a smell.

When the birds went he did miss them somewhat.
Still, there were no more bird-droppings
In his cooking pot.

Edible Fungi

In a muffled wood in a mauve gauze haze
The ground random and dumpy with cold winter days
Frilled up and frozen in brittle seas of ooze
Our dull footsteps
Crackle the plates of ice in muddy jars
The prints of horses' hooves.

In groups exotic the fastidious
Fungus has posed its small household
Tawynish pink and white
Graceful as sudden girls, fragile as shells
Or wings its dim gills
Gratuitously bodied out of night
Instant and frail this alien flesh
Ephemeral, from underneath the frost
And wet womb of the cold.
Now from the pan slimy as fish
Slithering darkly in their own ink
We eat water and earth.
A clean taste of blackness salutes the tongue.

Miss Beatrice May Baker

(Headmistress of Badminton School, Bristol, from 1911–1946)

Your genius was a monumental confidence
To which even the word 'courage' seems untrue.
In your *art deco* pastel ambience
You sat, *knowing* what to do,
Pure idealism was what you had to give,
Like no one now *tells* people how to live.

With your thin silver hair and velvet band
And colourless enthusiastic eyes,
You waved the passport to a purer land,
A sort of universal Ancient Greece,
Under whose cool and scrutinising sun
Beauty and Truth and Good were *obviously* one.

Upon your Everest we were to climb,
At first together, later on alone,
To leave our footprints in the snows of time
And glimpse of Good the high and airless cone.
How could we have considered this ascent
Had not our cynic hearts adjudged *you* innocent?

Politics too seemed innocent in that time
When we believed there would be no more war.
How shocked we were to learn that a small one
Was actually *going on* somewhere!
We lived through the jazz age with golden eyes
Reflecting what we thought was the sunrise.

And yet we knew of Hitler and his hell
Before most people did, when all those bright
Jewish girls kept arriving; they were well
Aware of the beginning of the night,
The League of Nations fading in the gloom,
And burning lips of first love, cold so soon.

Restlessly you proclaimed the upward way,
Seeing with clarity the awful stairs,
While we laddered our lisle stockings on the splintery parquet
Kneeling to worship something at morning prayers.
But did you really believe in God,
Quakerish lady? The question is absurd.

Music in Ireland

While we are hearing Mozart in this barn
Rain clatters on the roof
Which is made of corrugated iron
Or some such stuff.
Mozart can manage all the same
To elevate the noisy rain
Into a delicately lifted dome
Or ceremonial tent with glittering fringes,
Making it very taut and chill,
And people's clothes give off a clammy steam,
A somewhat awkward wet and woollen smell.
Afterwards there will be tea and scones
And dark blackcurrant jam
And a guided tour of the house.

We are in Ireland.
Murders are planned in time at certain hours
In homely kitchens when the meal is finished
By thoughtful men sitting beside turf fires
Over a drink with comradeship and wit,
Especially at weekends when leisure comes
For planting bombs, the weekly labour done.
Monday will bring again
The breaking of the news to families,
The life sentence of the child witness,
The maimed beloved in the wheel chair,
The condemnation to unending pain, and tears
Which have nothing to do with Mozart.

Nearby on Strangford Lough
Migrating geese bound for the Arctic Zone
Stand solemnly upon the glossy mud
In the brown twilight of the afternoon,
Soon to move on toward the midnight sun
With empty hills of snow to walk upon,
But now are waiting, dignified and sad,
Big heavy birds obedient to God,
Closely observed by the local bird-watching society
Against a misty background of factory chimneys.

Murder is abstract, something not imagined
In detail or defined as such,
Negating love and mercy, hideous
Schema of a detesting mind.
This music too is a material
That's not entirely human,
Instant and imageless as angels are,
Absolute in formation as the snow crystal,
Of necessity the aloof laughter,
Of undeserved delight the avatar,
Hinting the rhythm of the planet.
This is the matrix that we cannot fathom,
It is our response that is human,
Our restless yearning in the day's events,
Our temporal desire for resolution,
Our confused sense of a before and after.

Music lifts up like steam
The secret cares of hearers
Tired with cold and rain
And intermittent dream
Of their own sorrows and the old
Sorrows of Ireland
Which they try to banish.
Heads bowed down or thrown
Backwards open-eyed,
Here and there are dark
With terrible deaf pictures.
Sounds rise up and vanish
Into a pitted dome.
It continues to rain.
The acoustics being imperfect some people fidget.

Something which is pure has come
To a high magnetic field
Cry out as it passes on
When shall we be healed?

The Unpruned Pear Tree

The unpruned pear tree has put out
Some butterfly upwinged and white
And pink and few fugitive flowers
Riding upon the pale green tide of the May grass
Its skinny fingers tip and slide and pass
In the scant wind unfit for fruit,
Pretending rather some wild youth,
Some sudden stretching out toward the south
Toward the shining sun.
So the old tree dreams on.
Will it for this brief moment's beauty be
Forgiven, shriven?
What does it dream of, what remember,
If that a tree can think 'when I was young'?
It is so ragged foully huge and old
Come next November it will be firewood,
Made over into bits that can be stacked and sold.
Did it ever sweet pears give
And does it now refuse?
Dressed so in all its silken blooms it thinks to live,
Nor knows what fuel is, nor can conceive
Of windless rainless rooms.
Grieve it not now all winter's cold unleaving laws,
Hoping for some good, some renewal.
Fire for a tree is hell,
There is a vista where it fell.
How sweet the wood is burning now,
How sweetly these fruit branches smell,
The wood is green being the cause.

A Christmas Carol

The rich garb of the palace angels blinds
The honest shepherds' overburdened minds
So much so that they cannot see the portent
Simply cannot believe their eyes and do not;
While in the village other angels now
Embrace drunk unrepentant sinners who
Are startled to be hailed in Latin
By tall winged strangers dressed in satin.
Unauthorised cherubs dance upon the thatch
While down below excited sheep dogs watch
These teasing sprites, to whose jocund applause
They print the snow around with happy paws.
Pure songs of seraphim not heard on earth
Before resound to celebrate the cryptic birth
Where travails of entire creation bring
To us this helpless dangerous little thing.
Under arrangements made light-years ago
A long-tailed star divides the sky in two,
By day and night its burning river flows
Around the solitude of all that is.
Royal gifts glow under the dirty straw,
Three confused kings do not know what they saw,
Relaxed in their hotel discuss astronomy,
The Jewish problem and the Roman economy.
Great clapping wings of Spirit wrecked the house
Upon the day when Mary met her Spouse,
Between her trembling fingers nothing could be seen
Except an angel's white feet walking in the grass green.

Why me, thinks Joseph, all I wanted was a quiet life,
This Queen of Heaven Lady's not my wife,
And of the changeling brat I'm in loco parentis,
But will he let me make him an apprentice?
Since I am here I have to do it then,
The Infant thinks, surpassing thoughts of men,
With Father's help I'll get their sins in hand,
But really it's their suffering I can't stand.
So the Child knows that throughout endless time,
He will have his kneecaps shot off, be buried in lime,
Drugged into imbecility in mental homes,
Lie in deep oubliettes where no one comes.
Brought by the shepherd boys a little lamb
Lies panting quietly in fear and pain
With tightly tethered feet upon the stone
Beside a bright-eyed trussed-up speckled hen.

Macaw in the Snow

Snow falls on Gloucester Road and black
Processions of umbrellas bob
And penny-large the flakes rotate,
You in your cosy cage
Behind the window-pane hang upside down,
The pet-shop star, then amble to my tap
And tumble, eyeing me, and turn
A somersault – you are a clown!
Then spread a long amazing azure wing.
The snow-flakes weave their wool
Between me and my fool, while I
All spotted-white perceive you warm and dry
Scan me with saucy eye.
Cool scaly claw and sickle iron beak,
Bead of black tongue and witty eyes that speak
A gentle badinage,
While awkwardly the long tail-feathers sweep
About the gritty cage,
No room to fly.

I walk and leave you and I sigh
With sorrowful amaze
That our two spirits can identify
Simply by quiet gaze
I walk away and leave you and I sigh
Tears for your captive state.
Once in some netted green
Great wings astretch and conscious guiding tail

In sun-leaf-heat and river-steam
Gaily you were asail,
In your dim cage do you recall
Your Amazon and think it dream –
As goodness which we scarcely sense
Yet seems a place where we lived once
And we beguile our prison-doom
We clap our wings and play the clown!
Dear bright macaw in exile oh
Please pardon us the cage, the snow.

Iris Murdoch: Poet

An essay from the editors

'Poets can express much more than novelists, this connected sense of something which is simple and lucid and true and non-bogus and at the same time oddly accidental.' (Iris Murdoch, Interview with Jean-Louis Chevalier)

In the autumn of 2016, two of the editors of this volume were invited to search the attic of the home on Charlbury Road, Oxford, where Iris Murdoch lived for the last ten years of her life with her husband, writer and critic John Bayley. Audi Bayley, widow from Bayley's second marriage, kindly suggested to Anne Rowe and Miles Leeson that they explore the wealth of material abandoned there since Murdoch's death in 1999. There we found a small space patchily lit by a few exposed light bulbs, which lent an eerie quality to bulging cardboard boxes, battered suitcases and stacks of books, tilting alarmingly from the floor or spilling precariously from rickety wooden bookshelves groaning with the weight of multiple copies of Murdoch's novels. Two decades of dust had settled on gnawed plastic carrier bags out of which peeped the paws and heads of beloved soft toys. Others were full of chaotic swathes of handwritten manuscripts, one identifiable as that of her twenty-fourth novel, *The Book and the Brotherhood*, published in 1987. A battered suitcase, with which the Bayleys would have travelled the world, lay expectantly open on the floor alongside a picnic basket, providing a touching vignette of their contented domestic life. Paintings were randomly propped against walls and a life-sized portrait of Cloudy, the beloved Blue Merle Border Collie of her friend and authorised biographer, Peter J. Conradi, presided judiciously on a far wall, as if ensuring propriety and due diligence from these trespassers into her space.

Only gradually did an ancient oak chest, which could have been a relic from *Treasure Island*, come into view. In it we discovered ten notebooks of poetry, composed in Murdoch's distinctive hand and containing hundreds of poems, many revised repeatedly over decades. Alongside, nestled amongst pamphlets, photographs and random collections of letters, was a wafer-thin typescript of *Conversations with a Prince*, a poem cycle which Murdoch had sent to Norah Smallwood, her editor at Chatto, in 1963 and which, fearing it might be lost, she asked for its return some twenty-five years later. We discovered a copy here in her attic after another thirty years, and around sixty years after the poems were first written.

Murdoch's nagging insecurities about the worth of her poetry impeded its publication during her lifetime, even after she had become a household name as one of the most respected and prolific British novelists of the second half of the twentieth century. Her fame has remained rooted in her twenty-six best-selling novels that began with *Under the Net* in 1954 and included the James Tait Black Prize-winning *The Black Prince* in 1973, the Whitbread Book Award-winning *The Sacred and Profane Love Machine* in 1974 and the Booker Prize-winning *The Sea, The Sea* in 1978. In a poll by the *Sunday Times* in 1994, Murdoch was voted 'the greatest living writer writing in English'. Unbeknownst to most of her reading public, she was also a highly respected philosopher whose novels covertly merge gripping storytelling with serious moral philosophy. They are both compulsively readable and intellectually challenging – brave and open-minded, they situate the erotic and the sexual as defining aspects of human life. In their understanding of the anguish of gender confusion and same-sex desire, these novels demand tolerance and diversity at a time when homosexuality was still deeply taboo – even illegal before 1967. However, writing poetry gave Murdoch the freedom to explore her own confusions and compulsions that were being safely camouflaged in both her fiction and her public life.

The authenticity of feeling to be found in Murdoch's poetry is refreshing in the light of the sensationalised biographical accounts of her personal life that have dripped into the public domain. Three contentious memoirs by her husband appeared, the first in 1998, a year before her death, then in 1999 and 2001. They were followed swiftly in 2001 by Conradi's biography, *Iris Murdoch: A Life*, containing revelations of many lovers, male and female, which made headlines in the British press. Both then and since, the media's prurient interest has generated unfair and sometimes vindictive criticism of her lifestyle and dismissive assumptions about her marriage. The emergence of her poetry into the public domain gives unprecedented insight into the internal struggles that accompanied her many, often tortuous relationships which in turn inform the poignant psychological realism of her novels.

Perhaps because of Murdoch's own emotional struggles, the writing of poetry was an enduring and sometimes obsessive love although very little was published in her lifetime and has only been considered as tangential to her novels and philosophy. Moderate success first came with her juvenilia. In 1936, when Murdoch was a teenager, 'The Diver' was published in the Badminton School magazine, tellingly describing an intrepid young diver searching cold blue waves for a precious pearl enshrined in a silvery oyster shell. Two years later, two poems appeared in a charity anthology for which she had persuaded W. H. Auden to write a foreword. 'Star-Fisher', written as a jaunty ballad in the style of Charles Causley, hints at some frustration as the star-fisher's 'sense of vocation' is stifled by family who tempt her to 'cookery books' and 'knitted vests' – clearly not to her taste. Her first year at Oxford also brought some success when a selection of her poems appeared in university magazines, and she was now reading poetry ravenously. Marjorie Boulton, a fellow Somervillian, describes her giving an 'incredibly sound and startling penetrating critical study of Eliot, Pound, Auden, Spender, Day-Lewis and Louis MacNeice' at the Labour Club Study Group in 1942. A few years later, inspired by French poets including Breton, Valéry and Queneau, she furnished the bookshelves of her London flat with volumes of poetry of all eras and languages. By 1948 she was confessing to her Oxford friend David Hicks that poetry was obsessing her to the point that she was tempted to 'chuck' philosophy in its favour. Poetry remained close to her heart and always close to hand. More than fifty volumes were shelved in the studies of her Oxford and London homes, among them poetry by Roman, French, Greek, Russian, Jewish, Irish and Buddhist writers and numerous individual poets, including Shakespeare, Eliot, Yeats, Spender, MacNeice, Hopkins and Dylan Thomas.

Yet this fevered enthusiasm resulted in only two publications of her own poetry in her lifetime. *A Year of Birds* (1984) was originally conceived as a calendar with each short poem accompanied by a wood engraving by the celebrated engraver Reynolds Stone. A more substantial collection, published in 1997, was produced in Japan by Yozo Muroya and Paul Hullah in close collaboration with Murdoch herself, and included some juvenilia and a selection of poems which had previously appeared in a few relatively obscure journals. It was not until fifteen years after Murdoch's death that a further eleven poems, written to her one-time fiancé Wallace Robson, were gifted by Robson's son to the Iris Murdoch Collections at Kingston University Archives, and published in the *Iris Murdoch Review* in 2014. This dearth was partly the result of her tendency to measure her own poems against the brilliance of the great poets she loved and the work of her highly gifted friends whom she cherished. Among them was the poet Stephen Spender, with whom, along with Spender's wife Natasha, Murdoch and her husband holidayed for many years at their home in Provence. There, in what she called the 'Tennysonian dusk', the two couples would sit late, being regaled by tales of Spender's long association with Auden and his conversations with Yeats. She was once romantically enthralled by the French philosopher-novelist Raymond Queneau, but also somewhat envious and intimidated by his poetry which she 'imbibed' with delight. 'You are a marvellous poet', she wrote to him: 'I wish I could write poetry. I sometimes try'. By comparison, she believed her own work to be 'mediocre'. Nonetheless, for over fifty years, she determined to fail better, recrafting her poems over and over in private notebooks.

Such perfectionism meant that transcribing her poetry notebooks took a group of dedicated volunteers almost five years. The same poem would appear in multiple versions, sometimes written years apart, which brought distinct challenges in deciding which one most accurately represented the emotional intensity of the poem. These dilemmas were exacerbated by the increasing illegibility of Murdoch's handwriting which, clearly legible in her youth, became more erratic. Deciphering individual words could be frustrating, and occasionally amusing. Was Murdoch walking along a beach 'in vain' or 'in rain'? And why would a poem about Odysseus be situated in 'Norwich'? (After weeks of puzzlement 'Norwich' revealed itself as 'travail'.) The need to solve riddles and corroborate assumptions sometimes meant searching for a crucial line in another poem or an elusive donnée within a novel, or cross-referencing with one of Murdoch's many hundreds of letters. This task was often frustrating, but solutions would sometimes appear somewhat eerily when a particular book or letter would miraculously fall open just at the page we were seeking. The sombre serenity of scholarly archives contrives a kind of intimacy that lends itself to the enigmatic, and being immersed in the intimacies of others can conjure not only a convivial presence but also a chilly antagonism, as if we are being scolded for our intrusiveness. Either way, these poems, forged out of such sincere and obsessive graft, provide an insight into Murdoch's emotions that is not to be found elsewhere. They reveal both her passionate aspirations as a poet and intimate shades of her psyche that her other achievements dare not express. If art, as she suggests, provides 'a complete and powerful picture of the soul', it became clear that to fully understand the woman and the writer Iris Murdoch was, it is essential to understand her poetry.

Writing in her journal in 1947, she asks, 'which poets give delight? . . . One immediately thinks – the Metaphysicals. Marvell. Donne. Some Eliot? Browning? A world. A voice. There is some metaphysical unrest expressed in these strange worlds'. The form of Murdoch's own poetry is governed always by the deep personal emotion that drives it. She has a fondness for internal rhymes and irregular metre to provide intensity. She can switch with ease from the serpentine intellectual complexities of the Metaphysical poets to the brisk satire of Byron, while more personal poems can recall poets as formally varied as Emily Dickinson, W. B. Yeats and Gerard Manley Hopkins. 'Afternoon Tea with a Lady' is indeed joyfully inscribed 'Eliot, Eliot, Eliot', and Blake, she suggests, is 'another source of delight. Innocence. Simplicity'. The sonnet, the lyric or the ballad can be emulated or contorted to dislocate expectations and reimagine the possibilities of form. There is much variation in mood, and readers will find echoes of the solemnity of Tennyson or the nonsense verse of Edward Lear. Her nature poems bear traces of the ethereal beauty of the Romantic poets, who had captured her imagination as a young girl; after hearing Sartre speak in Brussels in 1945, she wrote that she remembered 'nothing like it since the days of discovering Keats and Shelley and Coleridge when I was very young!' A journal entry from 1948 notes, 'Reading Rilke and Shakespeare's sonnets . . . Indulging my emotions'. Her love of Greek mythology and her belief in the universality of its characters are more evident in her poetry than in any other form of her writing, and her knowledge of world literatures permeates her poems to add layers of meaning.

This engagement with the work of great philosophers, poets and novelists produces poetry which is not constrained by any distinct 'Murdochian' style. Invigorating invention rubs shoulders with moving homages to tradition as she continually experiments with ways of working different perspectives into a concise poetic form. It is perhaps not surprising then, as she was also a keen amateur painter with a love of the visual arts, that many of her poems (and a significant number of her novels) reference much-loved artworks, 'Thoughts Around Nash's Wild Stones' and 'Bayswater Tube Station (suggested by Stanley Spencer's Beatitudes of Love)' amongst them. Tintoretto's Annunciation was clearly in her mind when she wrote 'Child Prays', a painting that also found its way into her novel The Sacred and Profane Love Machine (1974), when Harriet Gavender learns of the infidelity of her husband

and 'remembered an Annunciation by Tintoretto in which the Virgin sits in a wrecked skeleton stable into which the Holy Ghost has entered as a tempestuous destructive force'.

Another way of understanding Murdoch as a poet might come from a targeted reading of her novels, where she borrows unashamedly from the emotive qualities of poetic lyricism which touches the truth of human emotions more succinctly than prose. She seduces her readers into responding with the heart as much as the mind, as allusions to myriad poems nestle unobtrusively within her plots, enriching philosophical implications and psychological realism – Marian and Hannah reading Valéry's 'Le cimetière marin' in The Unicorn (1963) or Hattie and Father Jacoby reading Mallarmé in The Philosopher's Pupil (1983), for example. Direct quotations from favourite poems often give insight into the inner life of a character. The black maid Pattie, in thrall to the demonic priest Carel Fisher in The Time of the Angels (1966), finds solace in 'the poetry which takes the place of the prayer which took the place of the poor defeated magic of her childhood', and heartbreakingly comforts herself with lines learned by heart from William Blake's Songs of Experience: 'Turn away no more. Why wilt thou turn away? The starry floor, the watery shore, is given thee till the break of day'.

Ample evidence of Murdoch's frustrated poetical ambitions is embedded in a small army of tormented poets who bestride the pages of her novels and sometimes express her own self-doubt: 'Was the poem any good', anguishes Muriel Fisher in The Time of The Angels, 'Could one really tell with one's own stuff? She was well aware of the golden glow of ideal intention which, for the artist, covers so often the achieved reality of his own art so that it is hard to see the contours of what he has done amid the shimmering lights of what he might have done'. But Muriel is also convinced that she ultimately masters her trade: 'She was no longer a scribbler down of random inspirations. She knew now how to work, steadily and for hours on end, like a carpenter or a shoemaker'. Like Murdoch herself, Muriel soldiers on. Occasionally Murdoch's own poems are assimilated into her fiction: 'A Fallen

Tree in the University Parks' is echoed in her short story 'Something Special', and 'Macaw in the Snow' makes a guest appearance in *The Book and the Brotherhood*.

Murdoch was staunchly proud of her Irish nationality, which would occasionally infiltrate her poetry to illustrate both the deep pride she took in her heritage and her distress at the country's political disunity. She was born in Dublin of Irish ancestry in 1919, but moved to London as a baby with her civil servant father and would-be opera singer mother. She unfailingly referred to herself as 'Anglo-Irish', or even 'profoundly Irish', and implausibly claimed in a letter to her close friend David Morgan that she had 'an Irish accent you could cut with a knife'. The opening line of her poem 'To Kathleen ni Houlihan' (traditionally an emblem of Irish nationalism), 'I would go back to Ireland', echoes the famous opening to Yeats's 'The Lake Isle of Innisfree': 'I will arise and go now', expressing the depth of Murdoch's own grief for a land whose 'brow is white with sorrow' and whose 'dearest sons are dead' – although the animated ballad rhythm seems to evoke hope and optimism. A later, darker poem, 'Music in Ireland', expresses pain at the political fissure within the country by contrasting the exquisite pleasure of hearing Mozart under a 'ceremonial tent' in a barn with the murderous bombings simultaneously being planned in homely domestic kitchens. As political unrest intensified in Ireland, she became wary of the effect on her imagination, fearing she might romanticise its tragedy. In this poem, such physical and ideological conflict encapsulates 'their own sorrows and the old sorrows of Ireland' that she herself felt so keenly. Another poem, 'Approach to Belfast', deals more emotionally with the divisions within the country and acknowledges her own anguished sense of belonging. Both anger and deep love for Ireland are deeply felt as her boat docks at Belfast and she is 'lapped in the green arms of the island / And all about me is Ireland'. The incredible beauty and indelible tragedy of Ireland are always embraced by her love.

There is a general consensus now that Murdoch is, to some degree, a philosophical novelist, although not one in the strictest sense that some earlier writers such as Sartre were. As stated in many interviews, she actively tried to avoid her philosophical views impinging on the structure of her fictional works. However, she often explicitly engages with philosophy in her poems: 'I must make poetry out of philosophy' she would write in her journal in 1969. Shortly before writing some of her most important philosophical essays, such as 'A House of Theory' and 'The Sublime and the Good' in the late 1950s, Murdoch wrote the poem 'Word Watcher', which captures the nature of her evolving relationship with John Bayley (whom she would soon marry), although with a number of other romantic liaisons running in parallel. The poem highlights their intellectual kinship, which relies more on what she termed 'high eros', the desire for love, goodness and truth, as opposed to 'low eros', the desire for sex, power and control that so deeply informs her poems about relations with other men. Here, the poet reflects on the impotence of words in the face of such a profound and ineffable reality: 'Deep in the wood I lie apart, / And know of words only the cries / And see the blur and not the wing'. And she wonders that words had been 'tame enough to say / The things that Kant and Plato knew'. She implores the words, 'Pause now, and let your silence say / What caught would be compelled to sing'.

This desire to capture the messy nature of reality, what Murdoch would term the 'thinginess' of existence, becomes more prevalent in her poetry over time. 'Forest Fire' (written for Julian Chrysostomides) opens with the claim that 'these are not the proper words nor is this communication', and here the disconnect between the poet and the language employed has morphed somewhat – there is much more unsurety and the ground we stand on is more unstable. A little later in this cycle comes the poem 'I Overcome Love', where the poet wrestles with Love as Jacob wrestled with the angel. In the third stanza, Love says, 'Come, come . . . in your philosophy / You like to argue that a human's power / Is measured by his deeds, not secretly / Concealed in faculties that never flower / In open skill. Not accidentally, / My dear, it's mine to crow and yours to cower!' Much like in 'Word Watcher', there is a struggle, but here the struggle is between the lover and the beloved. A poem of force, about domination and consent, it shifts between the low eros of desire and the need to attend to the true nature of the other. As when Moy escapes from the swan in Murdoch's novel *The Green Knight*, there is, in the last stanza, a god humbled and the power differential – and perhaps the fantasy – undone.

Most central to Murdoch's poetry are her own emotional struggles that catalogue her obsessive loves, her visceral remorse for sometimes cruel behaviour towards others and her attempts to find the truth of her own feelings. A note from her journal of 1968 reveals that she could be scathingly self-critical when looking back on her unquestionably colourful love life: 'Rooting in the oak chest . . . came on a set of diaries dating from 1945 onward . . . God! Hardly dare to look. Keep seeing references to Philippa, Elizabeth, Donald, Wallace etc. etc. Christ. Rather *awful* actually, this continuity of one's life. When seen all together, that business of falling in love with A, then with B, then with C (all madly) seems a bit sickening'. In her poetry Murdoch faces up to the sometimes shameful repercussions of such behaviour and her own paralysing guilt. The poem 'Musical Evening for Three', written in 1955, describes her emotional upheaval at a concert with two beloved friends, Philippa and Michael Foot. The music stirs memories of what she termed a 'quadrilateral tale' of partner-swapping that had occurred over a decade earlier – and deeply tarnished her close friendship with Philippa, a contemporary at Somerville with whom she shared a flat in London during the Second World War. In 1944, Murdoch had cruelly ended her relationship with Michael, having appropriated Philippa's 'satanic' lover, Tommy Balogh, as her own. In a letter to her one-time fiancé David Hicks, she acknowledged in herself a 'dangerous lack of decision and will-power where other peoples' feelings are concerned. A sort of paralysis . . . left me in state of utter despair and self-hatred'. In a letter to Philippa in October 1946, she wrote, 'When one has behaved as I then behaved to two people one loves, the hurt and the sense of guilt go very deep'. Finding comfort in each other, Philippa and Michael later married, though subsequently divorced, and while Murdoch's friendship with Philippa was revived, she experienced enduring remorse for the injury she had caused both parties. In 'Musical Evening for Three', the surprising banality of style appears to be a deliberate act of sabotage by the guilt that informs it, a refusal to transform behaviour so cruel into a thing of elegance and beauty: 'I had not thought such pain were possible / . . . It is the echo that is terrible – / To find one's spirit can be bent again / Into that old and agonising spiral'.

Such feelings of self-hatred expressed in her poetry can be mixed with a frisson of sadomasochism. During a tempestuous love affair with the literary scholar and critic Wallace Robson while Murdoch was teaching at Oxford, her journal of November 1951 records a deep ambivalence: on the one hand she acknowledges that he is 'increasingly precious to me' and that she loves his 'gentleness', but she is also attracted to his 'violence, wit, all a language I understand. We communicate perfectly'. In a letter to Robson written on the London Underground, she confessed, 'You are my ill and its cure'. This phrase would become the seed of the poem '*Tu es mon mal*', written in her journal and sent to Robson as a letter a few months later when they were briefly unofficially engaged. The darkness of their attraction is explored in this poem in which she confesses the extremity of her feeling that 'pierces you like love': 'You are the troubled and dark power counter / To which setting foot and knee I strain / Until I define myself in a rending pain'. This extraordinary poem catalogues deviant emotions that were to titillate her imagination and inform similar, compulsively punishing relationships in her novels, among them Morgan Browne's passion for the sadistic Holocaust survivor Julius King in *A Fairly Honourable Defeat* (1970). However, unlike her character, Murdoch had the courage to break free. Her demonic pact with Robson did not last, and by January 1952 they had parted. Her journal records, with some sorrow, that 'W.R. is the shadow of the great man I wanted to marry. I am the shadow of the great woman I wanted to be. We are a pair of shadows'.

Murdoch's complex sexual make-up, which involved relationships with both sexes, was unknown to her reading public during her life. Her bisexuality was revealed in Conradi's authorised biography in 2001, and subsequently referenced in her private letters published in 2015. Much quoted has been her letter, written in October 1967, to the Austrian logician Georg Kreisel, to whom she confided, 'I can't divide friendship from love or love from sex – or sex from love etc . . . I am probably not at all normal sexually. I am not a lesbian, in spite of one or two unevents on that front; I am certainly strongly interested in men. But I don't think I really want normal heterosexual relations with them . . . I think I am sexually rather odd, which is a male homosexual in female guise'. Poems from as far back as the late 1930s both illustrate and equivocate this complex self-analysis and suggest some disingenuity and obfuscation on her part. In her public life there were good reasons for concealment, including fear of social censure: 'It's no good being a female queer', she wrote in her journal in February 1968, a year after her letter to Kreisel, 'one must be a male one'. Two poems from the juvenilia section of this collection, written a year apart when she was just a teenager, suggest that even then she was aware of her strong attraction to women. 'Ballad', written in 1938, describes a yellow-haired young woman riding a snowy white mare, whip in hand, with 'blood on her spurs, all gleaming and wet', who has stolen the poet's heart and cannot be forgotten. A year later, the poem 'To a Girl with Yellow Hair' is haunted still by the memory of this girl, whom Murdoch had met after seeing Eliot's *Family Reunion* in 1939. Even then she understood both the taboo nature of such feelings and their undeniability: 'the curse / of vision belongs to few. Kinship / Has here a meaning – let not / Life snap the thread'.

Much of Murdoch's poetry both celebrates her bisexuality and lays bare her fear of it being discovered. In December 1948, she wrote a poem of intense erotic desire in her journal which she did not copy into her poetry notebook. It provides a candid record of her feelings for her friend and fellow philosopher Elizabeth Anscombe, who was Research Fellow at Somerville when Murdoch was teaching at St Anne's. At this time, she and Anscombe conducted what Murdoch described in her journal as 'three days of courtship'. Her poem to Anscombe begins, 'The dear and detailed dream of your carved head / Fills all the dim dimensions of my pain. / Your most intent desiring lips and eyes / Brim from the mirror where I ask my name'. This was a desire both dangerous and doomed. Murdoch noted in her journal that a mutual friend, Yorick Smythies, had warned her that any relationship between the two women, even a 'sentimental' one, would be Anscombe's 'ruin', and Murdoch acknowledges in her poem that her longing to 'possess' Anscombe 'is to desire your death'. The following day she wrote a panicked note in her journal: 'I need a strong box to keep this damn diary in. Probably I ought to destroy all the entries of the last three weeks. Why am I unwilling to??' Yet seven pages from this section of Murdoch's journal were finally excised with a sharp razor blade.

There were other intense female attractions in the late 1940s and early 1950s. A relationship with a female fellow Oxford tutor, Peter Ady, lasted several years, during which time the women holidayed in France together, and in 1952 Ady declared her love for Murdoch. She was displaced in Murdoch's affections, however, by another Oxford tutor, Margaret Hubbard, who ultimately caused Murdoch's resignation in 1963 by pressing her to leave John Bayley so that they could set up home together. Murdoch's involvement with the novelist, critic and campaigner Brigid Brophy was to supplant both these relationships after the women met when they competed for the Cheltenham Literary Prize in 1954 (Brophy won for *Hackenfeller's Ape* and Murdoch came runner-up with *Under the Net*). In the 1960s, Murdoch's love affair with Brophy, who was openly bisexual but also happily married, had a major intellectual and emotional impact on her life. But their relationship was fraught; Brophy could be scathing about Murdoch's novels and, emotionally, Murdoch was unable to fully commit in the way that Brophy wanted. In the poem 'For B who tried to persuade me of something in a somewhat Freudian metaphysical poem', sent to Brophy as a letter, Murdoch playfully but firmly sets out her stall in relation to what she would and would not commit: 'You want me female, then you want me male, / Or else hermaphrodite . . . Since something to your purpose in me lacks - / . . . I will be neither lock nor key nor wax'. Intruding on such sexual intimacies in Murdoch's poetry can feel uncomfortable, yet permits a unique insight into Murdoch's complex sexual identity.

When Murdoch deposited her *Conversations with a Prince* typescript with Norah Smallwood at Chatto in 1963, she told her, 'I would like one or two of these poems to have a chance of surviving'. Five of these poems, conceived between 1954 and 1959, were dedicated in Murdoch's notebook to 'J.C.' but the dedications were removed from the copy that she sent to Chatto. She was reluctant, perhaps, to risk bringing into the public domain her friendship with a female student, Julian Chrysostomides, that she had kept closely under wraps, and that even since Murdoch's death has not attracted biographical attention. Murdoch met Chrysostomides, who became a Hellenic historian, when she interviewed her for a place at St Anne's in 1951 and took her under her wing, particularly because she was a refugee from Istanbul where Greeks were facing persecution.

Murdoch's poems to Julian feast on moments when the two women would be held in a moment of unconsummated passion, although it seems that Murdoch would have liked the friendship to develop into something more. She records in her journal how '[Julian] gave me a beautiful shell. I wept, hiding my face "why do you torment me so?" . . . A very strong desire to embrace and kiss her. She felt this too. Then she gave me the shell, and I wept'. Julian's gift inspired the earlier of two poems, both entitled 'The Shell (with J.C.)', in which Murdoch interprets the shell as a symbol of their suppressed desire. She is careful to disguise Julian's gender in an untitled poem drafted in her notebook which opens, 'Julian is cross or he pretends to be'. This line became 'Now you are angry or pretend to be' in the final version of the poem.

Two poems, 'Reading of Palms' and 'Refusal to Sing', fizzle with unspoken sexual frisson, capturing painfully exquisite moments of mutual arousal in both women, who are 'a little drunk with poetry'. Such taboo-fuelled episodes that test moral rectitude were to inform the psychology in many of Murdoch's novels, in particular *The Nice and*

The Good (1968). The plot echoes the scandalous scenario of Bronzino's painting, *Venus, Cupid, Folly and Time*, depicting an incestuous moment of 'dreamy suspended passion before the spinning clutching descent' between mother and son, Eros and Cupid. This novel illustrates the paradox between the joyous life-giving force of erotic love and its potential for tragedy that so poignantly informs her poems to Julian. Murdoch's poetry was perhaps the only safe space where she could express her own complex sexual orientation and the emotional cost of its denial.

It is unsurprising that the emotional turmoil that accompanied the many relationships in Murdoch's life is recorded more viscerally in her poetry of these years than in other writings, and that her nuanced feelings for her many lovers appear here at their most revelatory. Also chosen by Murdoch for inclusion in *Conversations with a Prince* are two poems for Arnaldo Momigliano, an Italian Jewish refugee who was Professor of Ancient History at University College London. They became lovers in the early 1950s, and their shared love of Greek mythology finds its way into many of Murdoch's poems. The first, entitled 'Ravenna', suggests that the aphrodisiac for this and possibly her other relationships with highly influential men was as cerebral as it was sexual. The poem was written after visiting the city with Momigliano in 1954, where she was impressed not only by his knowledge and lineage but also by his sensitivity to beauty. She watches him, enthralled 'head thrown back . . . immobile contemplating a fresco'. Her liaison with Momigliano was one of many synchronous relationships, and a number of poems in this sequence that bear no dedication offer various possibilities for the literary sleuth. She was certainly still hankering passionately for Queneau at this time, although in only a few years was to marry John Bayley (a fact which made Momigliano furious).

The subsection of the *Conversations with a Prince* cycle that bears the same title as the full typescript explores the devastating influence of a significant intruder into Murdoch's relationship with John Bayley.

These poems evolve out of Murdoch's three-year entanglement and much longer obsession with the Nobel Prize-winning Bulgarian polymath Elias Canetti, whom she met around the time of the death of another polymath and poet Franz Steiner in 1952, a man whom she said she would have married. Canetti was at once brilliant, volatile and possessive, and for some years she was in thrall to him intellectually, emotionally and sexually. This intense relationship generated the series of sonnets personifying the sadomasochistic aspects of erotic love later included in the 'Conversations with a Prince' subsection of her typescript. She was also acknowledging the dark side of her relationship with Canetti in her journals at this time and on one occasion, worrying that Canetti might be angry with her, recalls a Dante poem 'where love has got Dante pinned down on the ground and has struck him once – and Dante says if you even raise your arm again I shall die of terror'. In the sonnet 'I Overcome Love', she directly echoes Dante's image of being floored by desire: 'Love was triumphant and he arched upon / Me like an eagle pinning to his prey'. In her journal of April 1953 she wrote, 'C. made love to me savagely, tearing my clothes off . . . I told him he was like a great gale, and I was a tree in the gale'. This sonnet from Murdoch's notebook was not included in the typescript sent to Chatto, but appears here because it illuminates vividly the subservience that fuelled her passion for Canetti.

While Murdoch's relationship with Canetti informed her comprehensive studies of obsession and power in her novels, her poems reveal the personal torment of a woman torn between her love for the kind and gentle man whom she will ultimately marry and the extremity of passion for the man she herself obsessively desires – and who, she fears, has the power to destroy her. 'Have I unloaded so my heart to one / Who was not Love but seemed to be?' she asks in 'I Seek for Love at the Carnaval'. And as 'the slave of monotonous feet / Following the same pattern every time', she attempts to find her way out of this labyrinthine trap in 'Love Keeps a Maze'. The recurring imagery employed in this cycle to describe the compulsion of this passion is of the great dark-winged figure of the black Eros. In Greek mythology Eros, the god of love and desire, was sometimes depicted with black-feathered wings, the son of Chaos, the primeval emptiness of the universe.

If the black Eros is deadly, Murdoch can also be self-mocking and comically aware of the absurdity of this self-induced state of servitude. In 'Love Visits his Traps', Love taunts her: 'What you again? / You were so wounded last time and so sick / When I released you, you were almost dead!' The victim replies, 'I lay in bracken and my blood and said / "My lord, you have a gun, despatch me quick".' The moment of levity is brief, though, and these poems often lament the lack of self-control for which she attempts to find an antidote in her moral philosophy and her novels. In the poems, she flounders and fears that the gripping talons of the black Eros will destroy her self-respect, infringe on her liberty and bring despair. The prescient sonnet 'I See Love in Bad Company' depicts an extreme situation in an extraordinarily pedestrian context. On a moonlit night on a lamp-lit corner, a familiar face emerges from within a crowd of ruffians, and she recognises Love, 'who did me harm'. With his wicked face, he evokes a chilling awareness of how her moral weakness might harm her reputation: 'don't beat me to my knees', she pleads. In the poem 'I Meet an Old Friend', where the narrator is distressed to see illness and dejection, she 'knew in that ruined face reflected / How these same years had altered me'. The image of a ravaged female face, guilty of sexual incontinence, haunted her for decades, and recurs in *The Book and The Brotherhood*, published some forty years later in 1987. The morally barren, sexually enthralled Jean Cambus, in the process of deserting a loving husband for the second time to elope with her former ruinous lover, David Crimond, makes up her face, once 'stern and calm', in preparation, and sees it now as 'a mad scattered convulsed face . . . her lower jaw moving compulsively, a faint growling in her throat'. Although it should also be noted that one of the only two poems in Murdoch's notebooks overtly dedicated to Canetti suggests his more benign emotional impact on her life: 'I am never with you; but roam

/ The land that is you, and find / There the leaning tree and the kind / Faces of flowers – and mind / A little less being alone'. The imagery here suggests that the bond between them went far beyond the mere sexual gratification that has come to define it biographically.

Whatever the actuality of Murdoch's tortuous relationship with Canetti, she chose to end the 'Conversations with a Prince' subsection of her typescript with the possibility of freedom and redemption. The first draft of 'Love Smiles upon Us', written not long before she married Bayley in 1956, embraces a more peaceful domestic version of love with her husband to be. On a walk in the 'cloven frost-embittered earth' they become aware of one who 'once with grievous rod / Made all my woe in years before you came', but who now smiles upon them and passes by. This is a different Love – 'a gentle god', and the final poem of the cycle describes the arrival of 'Snowdrops', indicating, 'Our sober knowledge that the earth must run / To lean into the bosom of the sun'. In her journal on 17 April 1956, Murdoch wrote, 'the other night I woke and wrote down: get to the place from which happiness and goodness lie in the same direction. I think perhaps I am now (with J.B.) in that place'. Although her journey was not to be easy.

Four poems in the *Conversations with a Prince* cycle are dedicated to Bayley and provide a unique glimpse into the day-to-day reality of what would be an unconventional marriage. 'Word Watcher' explores the inadequacy of philosophical language to catch the multitude of emotions that flicker through the experience of a second – making the claim that art comes closest to the truth. 'Picture on a Tablecloth' transforms the multi-layered experience of a second into a word-picture that serves as an eternal memento of their love: 'I want to make the moment still more mine. / So let me draw across the sleepy scene / The formal pattern of poetic thought'. But there was always of course an underlying intricacy to their relationship and 'Pine Branches' acknowledges, in the light of her complex emotional life, how difficult it was for any man to love her. Sharp brittle pine needles are emblematic of the only kind of love she has to offer, and 'puzzled in our separate beds', she pleads with

Bayley to 'reach toward me in the night'. Although there is a hint of emotional blackmail, as she promises the reward of 'perfume of a southern land' that will 'be with you till the light'.

However, the final poem dedicated to Bayley, 'Oxford to Paddington', although voicing yet another caveat: 'I am a peril to your innermost heart', beautifully evokes the depth of her love for him: 'Like a corvette in the Ionian Sea. / The gentle force that circles you and me / Is tender as the murmur of the south, / And yet as all-compelling as the north'. These poems confirm the extent to which, despite her polyamory, her desire for peace and stability was genuine and deep, and that her marriage was to be an emotional anchor that lasted until her death: 'Precarious the sphere in which we move, / And yet I could believe it without ending, / Fixed by a miracle of understanding'. Nonetheless, Murdoch's late poetry explores not only her yearning for an emotional home but also imaginatively resurrects the seductive charm of infidelity so intrinsic to the psychology of her novels. The psychological acuity of her poem 'Odysseus on Calypso's Island' humanises one of the most conflicted Homeric characters, who longs for his home and the love of his wife but is spellbound by the charms of the alluring goddess Calypso. Odysseus is trapped in infidelity behind the harsh line of the sea that symbolises the dangerous boundary where moral authority crumbles. He succumbs to the temptations of the island; Murdoch chooses the security of home.

The twenty poems that comprise the final section of this collection were written between 1972 and 1995 and range from personal reflections on Murdoch's childhood in her homage to 'Miss Beatrice May Baker, Headmistress of Badminton School', to fond memories of her beloved father in 'Avonmouth Docks', with whom she once said that she and her mother lived in a 'perfect trinity of love'. The insidious yearning for carnal love is recognised again in 'Edible Fungi' when, on a crisp winter walk through woods, she sees wild mushrooms grow in 'groups exotic' with 'alien flesh ephemeral' emerging from 'the wet womb of the cold'. Later, when they slither 'darkly on the tongue' with 'a clean taste of blackness' the serpent nestling in the soul is recognised, dormant and indestructible. Yet peace is also found in an enduring harmony with nature, a beloved companion throughout Murdoch's life. 'Colour Patches' is a Keatsian celebration of autumnal colours and birdsong in which the season of mists and mellow fruitfulness serves to 'unbind the bandage of anxiety', which can take on both personal and global form. 'Child Prays', on the other hand, counteracts the domestic peace she treasures with the cloaked image of the Holocaust and the prospect of nuclear catastrophe, world events of which a small child cannot hold any meaningful conception, but of which Murdoch herself is all too aware.

Both moving and fitting is that Murdoch's thoughts in these years turn to the memory of her early, chaste love for Frank Thompson, a fellow Oxford student who fell in love with Murdoch and saw her as his 'dream girl'. He joined the army in 1939 and was later recruited to the Special Operations Executive, a British organisation formed in 1940 to conduct espionage and sabotage in German-occupied Europe and aid local resistance movements. In charge of a mission in 1944, aged just twenty-four, he was executed in Bulgaria by firing squad. Still haunted by his death and fearing that her rejection of him fuelled an already reckless streak in his nature, her poem 'Agamemnon Class 1939' articulates her crippling agony at the senselessness of his death: 'and you / Are all pain and yet without pain / As is the way of the dead'. This poem was not conceived until the 1970s and Murdoch drafted many versions before its first publication in 1977. In her journal in 1978, she noted 'A dream about Frank. I was with Frank and he told me he loved me. (As he did on that day in autumn 1938 in New College)'. In her poetry she was free to express the brutality of her own losses and come to terms with her guilt. But this poem gives meaning not only to the futility of the death of Frank Thompson, but also to the deaths of all those slaughtered in the Second World War.

The last of the many fictional poets who walk the boards in Iris Murdoch's novels is Benet Barnell in her final novel, *Jackson's Dilemma*

(1995). His elegiac lament is surely a *cri de coeur* from Iris Murdoch herself: 'How I wish I had stayed in the light and devoted my life to poetry'. Without question, of all the art forms with which she experimented in her life, it was never having made her mark as a poet that caused the most regret, and camouflaged within the striving of her fictional poets are insights into her own aspirations and fears. In the closing pages of *The Sea, The Sea* Charles Arrowby ponders on what he should do with his recently deceased cousin James's unpublished poems and decides against a publisher in case the poetry turns out to be 'embarrassingly bad': 'Even if James is the greatest poet of the century he must wait a little longer to be recognised. I think he will have to wait until after I am dead'.

For better or worse, Murdoch's poetry, too, has languished until long after her death before being fully acknowledged. But shining a light on these poems from her attic has meant that it can be said with some confidence that her fears were misplaced. For there is true merit here, not only in the scourging of the soul *in extremis*, in her vast learning and in her deep appreciation of the natural world, but also in the artistry that characterises her tortured attempts at perfection. Perhaps the last words should go to Miles Greensleeve in *Bruno's Dream* (1969), one of several similarly tortured poets patiently striving in the shadows of her novels. Miles finally acknowledges, after years of attempting to process through his poems his grief at the loss of his beloved wife Parvati, that now 'he heard in poetry for the first time his own voice speaking and not that of another. And he knew that the moment had come at last when he could with humility call himself a poet'.

Anne Rowe, Rachel Hirschler, Miles Leeson, Frances White

Biographies of dedicatees

Stella Aldwinckle
Murdoch met Stella Aldwinckle, a representative of the Oxford Pastorate and founder of the Oxford Socratic Club, in 1941 when Murdoch was an undergraduate at Somerville College, Oxford. They remained friends and in 1990 Murdoch wrote the foreword to Aldwinckle's *Christ's Shadow in Plato's Cave: A Meditation on the Substance of Love*.

Elizabeth Anscombe
Murdoch and the leading twentieth-century philosopher Elizabeth Anscombe were fellow dons at Oxford in 1948 and remained in touch for the rest of their lives. Murdoch's *Metaphysics as a Guide to Morals* is dedicated to Anscombe.

John Bayley
Murdoch's husband, John Bayley, was a literary critic, novelist and distinguished Oxford academic. In 1950 he was awarded the Newdigate Prize for Poetry and in 1954 was elected Fellow of New College. In 1974 he became the first Thomas Warton Professor of English Literature there. Their marriage in 1956 lasted for over forty years.

Brigid Brophy
A bold and unconventional novelist, a critic and a campaigner for social change. Her relationship with Murdoch began when they met as recipients of Cheltenham Literary Prizes in 1954. The women became deeply emotionally involved in the 1960s and remained friends until Brophy's death in 1995.

Elias Canetti
Bulgarian writer and polymath Elias Canetti was awarded many prizes including the Nobel Prize for Literature in 1981. An acclaimed

intellectual, Canetti wielded great power and influence over Murdoch during the 1950s and their tempestuous affair had a profound impact on her life and work.

Julian Chrysostomides
Notable Hellenic historian Julian Chrysostomides left her home in Istanbul in 1950 where her fellow Greeks were facing persecution. After her initial attempt to study at Oxford was unsuccessful, Murdoch interviewed Chrysostomides for a place at St Anne's College to read Classics and became her tutor. They remained friends for the rest of Murdoch's life.

Philippa Foot and Michael R. D. Foot
Eminent philosopher Philippa Foot (née Bosanquet) and Murdoch were contemporaries at Somerville, where they established a friendship that endured until the end of Murdoch's life. Philippa's husband, Michael Foot, was a distinguished academic and historian. While a rift between Murdoch and Philippa was eventually healed, Murdoch remained distanced from Michael after he and Philippa were divorced.

David Hicks
Murdoch had a passing flirtatious relationship with David Hicks when they met at Oxford in 1938. Their friendship was resumed in 1945, and they were briefly engaged after he returned from his various postings with the British Council. Their relationship finally ended with Hicks's rejection in 1946, but their friendship endured for many decades after.

Arnaldo Momigliano
Murdoch and Arnaldo Momigliano, an Italian Jewish refugee who was Professor of Ancient History at University College London, became lovers in the 1950s. They shared a love of Dante and the ancient world, but their relationship suffered after Murdoch's marriage and their reconciliation followed only many years later.

Patrick O'Regan
An early boyfriend from Murdoch's Oxford days. Encouraged by her to move away from pacifism, O'Regan enlisted in the British Army in 1940 and was decorated for military service. He went on to have a distinguished career in the diplomatic service but died aged forty-one. His surviving elder brother believed that Murdoch gave him the courage and determination to fight.

Wallace Robson
A noted literary scholar and critic, Wallace Robson was Murdoch's lover at Oxford in the early 1950s. They were briefly unofficially engaged, but Murdoch ended their stormy relationship in April 1952. He published a volume of poetry, *The Signs Among Us*, in 1968. He left Oxford in 1970 to further his distinguished academic career.

'M.S.'
The identity of this dedicatee is unknown.

Sally – referred to in the title of the poem 'The Doves'
The identity of this person is unknown.

James Henderson Scott
A close friend of Murdoch's Irish first cousin Cleaver Chapman. In 1937 Cleaver encouraged Henderson Scott to write to Murdoch, believing them to be kindred spirits in their love of poetry and Ireland. A romance, by correspondence, ensued but did not develop after they eventually met in London.

Emma Stone
The daughter of the distinguished engraver and artist Reynolds Stone and the celebrated photographer Janet Stone. Reynolds's wood engravings illustrated Murdoch's poetry collection *A Year of Birds* in 1978. Murdoch and Bayley were regular house guests at the Stones's

home, the Old Rectory in Litton Cheney, Dorset, and were close to all their family.

James Meary Tambimuttu
Murdoch encountered the Tamil poet in the bohemian London set in the 1940s when he was editor of *Poetry London*. He published some of her poems in the *London Apple Magazine* in 1979.

Frank Thompson
Thompson studied Greats at Oxford, where he was captivated by Murdoch, a fellow student. She persuaded him to join the Communist Party, but he turned away from its ideology and left Oxford to volunteer for the British Army in 1939. On a Special Operations executive mission to Bulgaria in 1944, he was captured and executed by firing squad. His premature death had a profound effect on Murdoch who idealised him in her memory.

Select bibliography

Cheryl Bove and Anne Rowe, *Sacred Space, Beloved City: Iris Murdoch's London* (Newcastle: Cambridge Scholars Publishing, 2008).

Peter J. Conradi, *Iris Murdoch: A Life* (London: HarperCollins, 2001).

Gillian Dooley (ed.), *From a Tiny Corner in the House of Fiction: Conversations with Iris Murdoch* (Columbia: University of South Carolina Press, 2003).

Avril Horner and Anne Rowe (eds), *Living on Paper: Letters from Iris Murdoch 1934–1995* (London: Chatto & Windus, 2015).

Miles Leeson, *Iris Murdoch: Philosophical Novelist* (London: Continuum Press, 2010).

Priscilla Martin and Anne Rowe, *Iris Murdoch: A Literary Life* (London: Palgrave Macmillan, 2010).

Yozo Muroya and Paul Hullah (eds), *Poems by Iris Murdoch* (Okayama: Okayama University Education Press, 1997).

Anne Rowe, *Iris Murdoch: Writers and Their Work* (Liverpool: Liverpool University Press, 2019).

Frances White, *Becoming Iris Murdoch* (London: Kingston University Press, 2014).

Notes

'Thoughts Around Nash's *Wild Stones*'
Paul Nash, a British Surrealist painter, war artist and photographer was, like Murdoch, fascinated by the characteristics of natural stones. He created two artworks entitled *The Nest of Wild Stones*. The first, an arrangement of stones collected in 1936, was photographed by John Piper. Nash went on to paint a similar watercolour of stones, reusing the same title, the following year.

'He gave me a posy'
Guerdon (archaic): a reward or recompense.

'Bayswater Tube Station' (suggested by Stanley Spencer's
The Beatitudes of Love)
Stanley Spencer was an English painter whose work is a mixture of spirituality, religion and eccentricity. *The Beatitudes of Love* (1937–8) comprises eight paintings that examine themes of love, desire and infatuation, and which Spencer described as his 'couples' paintings.

'On a Head from the Acropolis' and 'The *Acropolis Korai*'
In her first version of 'On a Head from the Acropolis', Murdoch wrote alongside '(*Acropolis 643*)', identifying her subject as a beautiful head belonging to one of a group of statues known as the Acropolis Korai. This collection of ancient, pre-Classical, Archaic Greek female statues was damaged in the destruction of the Acropolis during the second Persian invasion of Greece in 480 BCE. The statues were buried by the victorious Greeks beneath their rebuilt citadel and preserved there for many centuries until their excavation in the late nineteenth century.

'Tu es mon mal'
Translation of final stanza:

Tu es mon mal oh toi mon guérison,
Tu es la froide terre que reveillaient mes pleurs,
La mort qui me venait combleé de fleurs
Dont le parfum est enfin un bénison.

You are my suffering oh you my healing,
You are the cold earth that my tears awoke
The death that came to me filled with flowers
Whose scent is finally a benediction.

'You by Telephone'
Nam sine amore gravi femina nulla dolet.
Quotation from Propertius's poem 3.8:
'For without serious love no woman suffers pain.'

'I Seek for Love at the Carnaval'
Murdoch uses the spelling 'Carnaval', an archaic form of 'carnival'.

'Agamemnon Class 1939'
The word 'Medize' (in ancient Greek history) means to side with the Persians; to be loyal to the Persian Empire rather than the Greeks.

Details of previously published poems
'The Diver': first published in *Badminton School Magazine* 69 (Spring term 1936).

'Star-Fisher': first published in *Poet Venturers: A Collection of Poems written by Bristol School Boys and Girls*, ed. by Iris Murdoch (Bristol: privately printed, 1938).

'*Tu es mon mal*'; 'The trailing stars tell of dooms'; 'I find that honesty is a hard thing'; 'You ask a hundred sonnets of me'; 'There is no flower on the asking tree': all first published in ' "Raids of the Inarticulate", Poems for Wallace Robson' (with an introduction by Frances White and a preface by Hugh Robson), *Iris Murdoch Review* 5 (2014).

'For B, who tried to persuade me of something in a somewhat Freudian metaphysical poem': first published in *Living on Paper: Letters from Iris Murdoch 1934–1995*, ed. by Avril Horner and Anne Rowe (London: Chatto & Windus, 2015).

'John Sees a Stork at Zamora': first published in *Boston University Journal* 23.2 (1975).

'Agamemnon Class 1939': first published in *Boston University Journal* 25.2 (1977).

'Poem and Egg' and 'The Brown Horse': first published in *Transatlantic Review* 60 (June 1977).

'Motorist and Dead Bird': first published in *The Listener* 97.2513 (June 16, 1977).

'Fox', 'No Smell' and 'Edible Fungi': first published in *Poetry London / Apple Magazine* 1.1 (Autumn 1979).

'Miss Beatrice May Baker': first published in *People: An Anthology*, ed. by Susan Hill (London: Chatto and Windus/Hogarth, 1983).

'Music in Ireland': first published in *Occasional Poets* (London: Viking, 1986).

'The Unpruned Pear Tree' and 'A Christmas Carol': first published in *Something Special: Four Poems and a Story* (Helsinki: Eurographica, 1990).

Facsimile of draft of 'The Unpruned Pear Tree' from Iris Murdoch's poetry notebook.

Acknowledgements

We are grateful to the dedicated group of volunteers who, along with the editors, transcribed the poems from Murdoch's ten poetry notebooks found in the attic at her home in Charlbury Road, Oxford. They include Lucy Oulton, Julian Way, Deirdre Wilkins, Christine Wise and Sally Wood. Xavier and Rupert Villers and Hannah Driscoll generously facilitated access to much other related material at Charlbury Road since the death of Audi Bayley in December 2024. Kingston University Archivist Dayna Miller and her collections team colleagues efficiently provided extensive access and detailed information since Murdoch's poems arrived at the archives in 2016. Peter J. Conradi patiently answered our queries and offered valuable help and information. Norah Perkins from Curtis Brown gave greatly valued specialised support and advice. Annette Badland, Avril Horner and Stephen Lehec were proficient and insightful readers of first drafts of the editors' essay and we are grateful to each for incisive comment and suggestions. Avril Horner also helped with French translations. Emma Pytel and Louise Andrews, teachers at Kingston Grammar School, assisted with queries on Latin and French translations, and also Greek history. Paul Hullah advised on early choices of individual poems to be included in this collection, and we are grateful for his guidance and support. Daniel Read patiently helped with a variety of queries and provided excellent proofreading skills. Pamela Osborn undertook enlightening early research on individual poems. Nigel Rowe's and Ben Hirschler's practical help has been much appreciated. Heather Robbins at the University of Chichester provided supportive administrative assistance. Finally, we are indebted to the expertise of Rosanna Hildyard and Sarah Howe, our editors at Chatto & Windus, and to Sam Stocker and Leah Boulton for their meticulous copy-editing.